Scattered Letters

A Novel

By

Reshunniece Kline

Chapter 1

Spring came, bringing clear blue skies, melted snow, blooming floras, and smells of citrus. I was filled with joy, knowing my parents and I could spend our mornings outside, by the garden behind our home. In Geneva, spring was a beautiful season. "Bellina, the sun is shining, my love." My mother woke me as soon as the sun rose high. She was a woman full of grace. She floated as she walked and became a ballerina when she danced. She sat nobly secure as she ate her cuisine in the order of the fork; other people stopped eating to evaluate her, deciding where she came from. What were her mysterious set of green eyes saying? Words came out of my mother's mouth like a lovely song, as she spoke in French or Italian.

Her eyebrows went up and down when she stressed a word, making her more mysterious. I often imitated her acts. I had her features, long straight jet black hair, light brown tone skin, high cheek bones, and ruby red lips, but I was clumsy like my father. I think that's what my mother loved about us; we weren't perfect.

"Bellina, get dressed. We'll see you outside." She left the door cracked. I got out of bed, rubbing the sleep from my eyes. The poem my mother gave me, on my nightstand, greeted me.

> *There are doves that fly*
> *Some that will die*
> *Those who fly bloom*
> *Those who don't loom*
> *These are the paths we must make*
> *In time, which one would you take?*

It was something my grandmother told my mother and my mother told me. I repeated it every morning; it made me feel closer to the grandmother I never knew. My father didn't like my mother's parents. He was even more upset we lived in my mother's childhood home. I did not mind as much. My father was a tall, handsome, and crazy man from Syria. He had green eyes, black hair, and fair skin. Women thought he was a model, until he would walk into something. We worked on his car in the mornings, a red '67 mustang. I didn't know why he had one; he rode his bike everywhere he went.

"Bellina, this car is made of gold," he said proudly. When he opened the hood, I wondered which parts were made of gold, because all I saw was rust. He showed me how to change the oil, a flat tire, how to wash and shine a car.

"Mornings are the best time to work on your car. The air is always fresh. See; look at the flowers blooming over there." My father directed my face to a small patch of flowers in the front of our neighbor's house. During our breaks from the car, we would lay our backs on the grass and watch earth awaken.

It was the most beautiful site I'd ever seen. My mother would prepare fresh coconut cakes topped with mango sauce, flat cakes, and poached eggs. She would serve orange juice and berries, with a little sugar sprinkled on top. I sat in the middle, as my mother and father conversed about politics, gourmet foods, schools, and other things circling over my head.

Sometimes, the three of us would dance together. My mother would pull away. "I can't stand the smell of you two anymore," she joked. She wore a white and pink floral sun dress with black sandals. "I'm going shopping for some bread." She went her way while, my father and I stayed.

"Bellina, you're a beautiful girl. That's what your name means. It means beautiful girl." He looked me in my eyes. "I can't tell you enough how much I love you. You're my beautiful girl. See this place? This land is ours. If I'm not here, it's up to you to walk through the garden and work on the car." He smiled and kissed me. He clipped something in my hair. I tried to see what it was.

"Take it off when you go to bed." Later that night, I unclipped the clip from my hair. The hair clip had purple and green crystals shaped like a butterfly. I fell asleep to the music my parents were listening to with my clip in my hand. Every Wednesday night, my mother had friends over. They would gossip about New York. I never paid attention to their conversations.

"You know, Amelia, since I've been in Geneva, I've been attracted to mother's nature and all of its promises and beauty," my mother's friend would broadcast.

"Yes, yes, I know, Claudia. Tell us just how did you manage to crawl from the gutters of Brooklyn to upscale Manhattan to glamorous Switzerland?" my mother teased. Claudia had shown me pictures of her upbringing. My mother and Claudia went to college together. She came from nothing but a box. Her mother died of cancer and her father became a drunk. She and her siblings were homeless by the time she was twelve.

"We were the kids with the cups in our hands on the sidewalks. The easiest way to get money was for my brothers to break-dance. We always got money that way," she reminisced. She talked about how people would belittle them and walk right past her. She wanted nothing more than to be noticed. She applied to college and was accepted.

"Well, my dear friends, I became one of them. I became one of the elite," Claudia proudly stated. There were several other people there; Claudia's husband had to work. He and my father were partners at the bank. On the evenings, my mother would serve wine, cheese, and fruit. I was served fruit juice. At my bedtime, Claudia tucked me in. She sat on the side of my bed.

"I had another dream," I consoled to her.

"What happened this time?" Claudia's voice always smoothed me. Her soft tone made me feel safe to tell her anything. "I was swimming in a pile of letters."

"Letters? Hmm, that's a new one." Claudia held on to my hand.

"Yes, it was like I was drowning in them."

"With dreams, sometimes it's best if we let the dream play out, so we can get to the end and have it be over. It's only a dream, nothing can hurt you," Claudia assured me, moving back her blonde hair from her face. She was tall, curvy, and had small brown eyes and thin lips. She wasn't beautiful, but she had a personality that attracted men from everywhere.

"Try and get some sleep, dear. Tom and your father should be here soon." She kissed my forehead. Then left my door cracked, so I could hear my father coming in.

"Bellina, I'm home," my father yelled. I dodged out of my bedroom and into my father's arms.

I stayed up late to hear stories about why my father went to college at NYU to see how the American girls were.

"I heard they were pretty, tall, and easy," I overheard him tell Tom once.

"Papa, what's easy?" I asked him.

"Easy is to take out to dinner, court," my father explained, blushing slightly.

I looked up at him with confusion. "What is to court?" I requested a better explanation.

Tom laughed and called me a little reporter. "Will you please sign me an autograph, I want to say I knew you when you were a little person, before you made it as a reporter for the BBC."

My father smiled at me and pulled me closer. "It's how I got your mother. See, I saw this beautiful girl at a dance hall. It was early May, the night was beautiful. She stepped out of the crowd wearing this red silk dress. She had curly black hair, beautiful skin; her full lips lay upon a beautiful smile. She wasn't very tall; her piercing green eyes made up for it. She was the devil in the red dress; I had been searching for her. I ran outside. Luckily, there was a floral shop next to the dance hall. I went in and bought a dozen of lilies, clear aqua and lavender." My father then pulled out lilies from behind him for me. They smelled like they were picked from a fresh pond.

"I do believe lilies are sensual to a woman," my father added while glancing briefly at my mother.

"Papa, what's sensual?" I solicited, not knowing the depth of my question.

"Shhh, shhh, shhh, I went back into the dance hall and went straight to her, handed her the lilies. I whispered in her ear, would you give me the pleasure of dancing with you?"

"You're happy she said yes, huh?"

"You bet these two feet I am. Tell me, how are your dancing shoes lately?"

Before I could answer, he swung me up and placed my feet on top of his. We danced across the living room all evening while mother cooked. He told me about New York and his non-heated apartment, which made the winters brutal. He sat in his huge navy blue arm chair, stomping his foot and slapping his knee from laughing at his own stories, amusing me. We watched the evening news; my father loved the BBC because they tell it like it is. Whenever he didn't like the way men were acting, he would slap his knee and say, "He's acting like an ass! Bellina, don't marry an ass! You're too good for that."

My father was murdered on September 28, 1985, a day after my ninth birthday. That morning he went to open the bank he and Tom owned. A man, Jean-Luc Marrio, came behind him and shot him twice in the back. The man ran, but later was detained. Geneva had always looked beautiful year round; today it was windy, with a few raindrops.

It wasn't beautiful at all. The sky was dark, with a few white clouds. Thunder rolled like an angry lion. People were everywhere in our home, mostly friends and co-workers. They dressed in light colors because my mother thought it would be better to celebrate my father's life.

Some celebration; I went into my parents' room. Ocean paintings with white sands hung on the wall. The rocking chair was in the corner next to my parents' unmade bed. My mother hung on the rustic dresser my father made for my mother. She sobbed, putting her arms around me.

"I'm so sorry, sweetie." She turned me to look at her, "You know your father loved you very much." She went to stare out the window, holding herself, slowing rocking back and forth until she couldn't hold it anymore breaking down and crying.

"Bellina," Claudia called me from the door. "Honey, come help me make supper." She waved me to her.

"Are you going to be okay by yourself?" I asked my mother. I never wanted to leave her, as she sat in silence.

The first four months after my father's death were difficult. The man who murdered my father used insanity as an excuse. He invested in my father's bank when it first opened. He had misused his savings and lost all of it. He asked my father for a loan, but my father turned him down. The man said he couldn't go home to his wife and children with no money. The man was sure his wife would leave him. So, he waited for someone to come to the bank. He only wanted to threaten him, therefore he brought a gun.

"It was something out of my control. I became someone else. Before I knew it, I fired … again … again … again, than I ran," he explained. "My client was frightened and under duress. Therefore he can't be held responsible for his actions," his lawyer defended. I put down the newspaper. I flew up in rage. Everything I touched in my room went flying in all directions.

"What are you doing?" My mother stood in the door, "Bellina!" She rushed at me, with her arms open.

I balled my fist tightly, shaking them in the air, "Noooooo!" I screamed, crushing my jaws tight enough to cut my gums. I threw myself out of my mother's arms and ran away. I ran outside to the garden, falling onto the ground, screaming.

"Bellina, we'll be fine, everything is fine." My mother threw herself on me. We both lay on the ground crying. Not long after, down came the rain and we cried harder until we fell asleep on the ground in the rain. Soon, it was winter and the garden hid under the snow. The sky was blue and the ground was white. It looked like a scene from a fairy tale book. The leaves on the trees turned to icicles; the animal coats blended in. My mother ran into the house and grabbed what blue and purple lilies we had.

"What are you doing?" I ran after her.

"Come, Bellina," she said as she drifted out the door, forgetting her coat. I ran barefoot after her, still in my night gown. We threw the lilies everywhere and twirled with our arms in the air. I felt like the swan in Swan Lake. My mother began to dance; I copied her moves. The snow began to fall.

"Swan Lake captured my heart. It is the most romantic ballet I've ever danced to," she enlightened me by the fireplace in our living room. By spring everything was back to normal. We inherited a vast amount of money and a considerable amount of land. My mother gave my father's share of the bank to Tom. I received new school uniforms in maroon, tan, navy, plaid skirts with white blouses. My black dress shoes had a buckle, my stockings had patterns. I also had a gray and black blazer and many different sweaters.

"Can I get some casual clothes, too?" I pleaded.

"I don't know. You have some casual clothes at home, don't you?"

"Yes, I have uniforms at home and still got new ones," I pointed out.

"You're too smart for me. Go and get what you like," my mother surrendered easily. I picked out some sporty ensembles for which my mother nodded with approval.

Claudia visited often. She greeted my mother with a kiss, then me in the same way.

"Bonjour, ma belle fille, comment allez-vous?" she asked me in French.

"*Bonjour Claudia, je suis bien, et vous*?" I replied.

"Très bon, I bought you something."

"It's a coin from Brussels. It's one of the shiniest you ever bought me," I reported with giddiness.

"Yes, it is."

"What is it like?" I inquired. Claudia always traveled. She'd been to America, Kuwait, Italy, France, England and any other place a person could imagine. The stories she told were amazing. She was a journalist. On one of her trips to Syria, she stopped in a shop to buy something to eat. The menu board read *tea, coffee, cakes, salad and ass sandwiches*. She always would tell a story of this trip.

Her eyes wandered from the list and then came back to it. The young man behind the counter looked at her and said, "You look hungry, Ms. I'll get you one of our ass sandwiches."

No, no, no! I don't eat ass." By this time she had a lump in her throat. She wanted to run as fast as she could out of

Syria. The young man glared at her
confused. "Ms., the ass sandwiches are
beef, turkey, and we're out of egg. Which
one would you like?" I was so embarrassed.
It turns out ass mean assorted. We always
loved hearing that one and a million
others.

"What did you see in Brussels?" I
asked with doe-eyes upon my face. We made
tea, small sandwiches, and almond cake. My
mother and Claudia would tell me about
their travels. Claudia talked about her
many affairs and my mother would add
details that she remembered.

"Mother, before you met father, did
you have anyone else to love?" Curiosity
overcame me.

"Your mother was the hottest catch
in town. Men flocked to her feet," Claudia
said laughing.

"Oh, stop that." My mother paused and
winked at Claudia. "There was one. Thomas
was his name. He was the captain of the
soccer team. I always had a crush on him.
He was tall, blond, blue eyes, skinny,
cute."

"What happened?" I wanted to know.

"He had eyes for Claudia and now
they're married." They looked at each
other and laughed. From how my mother
described him, Tom was handsome. Now, Tom
was fat with thinning hair, but he had the
kindest heart. I laughed, thinking about
his weight gain. I guess he couldn't
resist Claudia's cooking. Life was slowly

settling down; it would never be normal. I sat in my father's car; not to cry, just to feel close to him. My mother came to join, siding in the passenger seat, the sun ending its work for the day, hitting the red paint of the car as it went down.

"How would you feel if I took a job working for the government as a translator?" my mother asked.

"I'd like that. If you do, will we be able to still spend our mornings in the garden?" My voice cracked with worry.

"Yes, yes, if we miss a morning, we'll just make it up on the weekend," my mother assured. She spent the whole summer working on her language skills and grammar. We had to go through regular dialogues; one for greeting, one for evening conversation, both formal and informal. We'd change the names of the people in the dialogues and start over.

"Before you go to school, we're going to take a trip to Paris and Milan. I think we can learn the language better and the cultures if we visit there," my mother stated.

We took a train to Paris. I sat by the window with my butterfly clip shining in my hair. I saw lands of green and rows of mountains. The mountains looked like they touched the sky. I couldn't keep my eyes from looking out the window. We stayed at a hotel near the Eiffel Tower.

After relaxing the first night, we went to the *Arc de Triomphe* and the Eiffel

Tower. We took our time to explore, eating at almost every restaurant. In the streets, we saw a show of comedies. They were climbing on chairs that were stacked, keeping us laughing. Our last week was in Milan. We woke up early to get to the boutiques.

In the evening, we were going to an opera. My mother knew what she wanted to wear and what I shall wear. She picked out a red silk dress that bared her shoulders. It was short in the front and had a tail. She wore black heels. Her hair was in a fancy bun, with dark makeup and red lipstick. She had black jewels around her neck. She looked stunning. I wore a silk dress that was fluffy and long. It was candy pink with a black sash. I had black shoes with a gold necklace. My hair was curly. I wasn't allowed to wear any makeup, only glitter on my neck and my arms. I was a princess.

We got out of the taxi and were swept into a circle of ladies and gentlemen dressed in long ball gowns of beautiful colors, draped with fine jewels, on the arms of black, sharp press tuxes. The gentlemen smiled at the ladies and commented to each other. It was a fairy tale we entered. Two grand glass doors opened, everyone entered the theater after our ticket was stamped. I was amazed how breathtaking the theater looked; colors of gold and red painted it.

There was a bar for refreshments on each side. We took our seats, the music started. The drama the actors brought to the stage, made me sit on the edge of my seat. The royal red velvet curtains made my heart salute the decor.

"Who's the woman singing?" I asked. My mother was so in toned to the performer she didn't hear me.

"Mother, who's the woman singing?" I asked her again.

"She's the prima donna," my mother whispered. This would be our last special moment together.

We were in a huge building. Government flags greeted us on the way in. "Bellina, stay close to me, I don't want you to get lost, " my mother instructed. my mother had an interview to be a translator. I waited in the lobby. People filled the place, wanting to speak to a translator, people who needed and wanted help. She rushed toward me, wearing a huge smile. I was proud of her; she got the job. We were happy; life seemed to be on track.

I woke up to the sun shining over my face. I pretended to be asleep, just in case my mother was on her way to wake me. I laid there and waited, wondering what she could possibly be planning. I heard doors closing, kept my eyes closed. No one came; I sat up and went to the door. I opened it and heard Claudia's voice.

"What are we going to do?"

I heard a mysterious voice instruct Claudia. Then I heard Tom's voice. I heard all these people in our house, but I didn't hear my mothers' voice among them. I walked to the stairway and saw Tom leading Claudia to an emergency van. There were police officers standing in our doorway. They saw me and stopped talking.

"You must be Bellina Al-Asma. I'm Marc Cortez." No one was smiling. "Bellina, that's a pretty name."

"Where's my mother? She wasn't here to wake me up."

"Something happen to your mum… uh, mother." He looked at me.

"Your mother, she passed away this morning."

My heart began to beat fast, then faster and faster. I felt the final beat, an explosion of my heart. He took my hand and I looked at his mouth. He was talking but the words became smaller and smaller until I couldn't hear him anymore.

"Bellina, hi honey, I'm Marie-Anne Levine. I'm the social worker Mr. Cortez told you about." Mrs. Levine smelled like she put triple doses of strong perfume on. I coughed and tried to pull myself from her scent. She had strings of gray in her hair, with a thin face. Her lips were painted with red lipstick that she managed to get on her teeth.

"Where's my mother?" I demanded with wide eyes.

"This is going to be hard for you, but I know you're a strong girl," Mrs. Levine revealed.

I stood there confused, not knowing what to do or say. My stomach grumbled only I wasn't hungry.

"Where are Claudia and Tom?"

"Unfortunately they're at the hospital. I'll stay with you until they come back," Mrs. Levine stated.

We sat on the stairs until Claudia and Tom came back. Mrs. Levine didn't speak. She looked straight ahead. Time went by, I felt like they left me, too. Claudia and Tom came home later that evening. I hadn't moved from our front steps. I didn't care that Mrs. Levine went to sit inside hours ago.

"Oh, Bellina." Claudia sat beside me with her arm around me. I could only cry in her lap. I knew I lost my mother. I was too weak to be angry. I cried until I smelt Mrs. Levine's perfume floating around us.

"Go on. Go to your room." Claudia lifted me. I pretended like I was obeying, but then I hid at the top on the landing next to my room. I could hear tired voices speak below me.

No one was prepared; we were unprepared for the loss of my mother.

"I don't want Bellina to know."

"She has the right to know what happened to her mother."

"What happened to her mother? She's only a little girl. I won't have nightmares put into her head." Claudia began to cry. I ran to the bed and buried my face in the pillow, screaming and crying. Why couldn't God take me, too?

Mrs. Levine came the next day, I stayed in bed.

"There's no will explaining what to do with the child, if anything were to happen to her parents. She belongs to, she belongs to us now. I'm sorry." Mrs. Levine stated. I heard Claudia's stifled cries becoming unbearable to contain. The sound made round teardrops roll down my cheeks.

"We will fight for her!" argued Tom. His words made me sit up and squeeze my pillow. I knew Tom meant it. He and Claudia would fight for me. I was shaking and praying to please let me sleep in my own bed. I didn't want to leave. I held on to my butterfly pin and lay back down.

The court date came faster than we thought. We were ready to stand up to the judge and anyone else who thought we shouldn't be together. We were put in a plain white room. We sat on one side; Mrs. Levine sat on the other, with two men sitting next to her. The room was intense. Claudia and I were holding hands under the table. When the judge came in, he ordered me to be escorted out of the room. I looked at Claudia and Tom, and their eyes told me it was alright. Mrs. Levine looked at me. She was a cold woman, I thought. I

left with the guard. I was in a children's
room when Marc came in.

"Bonjour, *petite dame*, how are you
doing?"

"Okay. Do you think they are going to
take me away from Claudia and Tom?"

"You certainly do not waste any time,
do you?" Marc said with a slight chuckle.

"I would like to know. They're the
only family I have. They are my family."

"Have you forgotten your parents?" he
asked. He paused and realized the
absurdity of that question. "No, they're
always in your heart. If somehow you can't
be with Claudia and Tom, then you must
always keep them in your heart."

"I hope we are able to still be
together."

"Of course you do, *petite dame*," He
shook his head in agreement. We started to
play some games. It took four hours before
the door opened. Another guard dropped his
head in and waved Marc to come with him.
Five minutes later they came back in with
Mrs. Levine.

"Bellina, we are going to your house
so you can pack some things to come with
us. You will be able to pack two
suitcases. The rest of your things will go
with Claudia and Tom." She stood in front
of me like a solider. There was nothing
kind about her.

"Sometimes the law is not fair, but
we must go on," Mrs. Levine bluntly told
me. She began to lead me through the door.

Marc walked by my side and Mrs. Levine walked behind me. As I turned the corner of the fluorescent hallway, Claudia and Tom were standing with forlorn faces. Claudia blew me a kiss, waving goodbye. I did not gesture back. I just left with Mrs. Levine.

I packed all I could possibly fit into the two small suitcases they provided me with. I convinced myself that it was okay to leave my parents' favorite things. Tom and Claudia would take care of them until I could come back to get them. I waited for Mrs. Levine to get off the phone. "Where am I going?" I asked.

"You have an aunt."

"No" I told her.

"Yes, she lives in New York," Mrs. Levine notified me.

"No" I told her.

"I am afraid so. You did not know your mother had a sister?"

"No … NO! NO! NO!" I knew at that moment that she was a liar. "No, no, no, do not lie to me! You have been lying to me this whole time!" I was enraged; she didn't know my mother. My mother wouldn't lie to me, let alone not tell me about a sister. I ran outside to stand on the steps. Mrs. Levine followed me and stood in the front doorway. I screamed at her as loud as I ever had in my life.

"Leave me alone!" She remained calm despite my visible fury.

"Her name is Michelle Hosset. Your mother's maiden name is Hosset. We have called her and she would be delighted to have you stay with her. She lives in New York. It would be a wonderful way for you to start fresh, meet new people, especially an aunt you never knew you had. You will be able to experience the city life." She tried to talk to me, but I didn't listen. The van came to take me; I refused to go.

"Bellina we are ready to go," she called me. "Bellina, please come," she called me again. Two men walked toward me. They advised me that I could come on my own or by force. I grabbed onto the pole of the steps.

"Okay, I guess you've made your choice," one of the men muttered, then they both came at me. One took me by my legs and the other grabbed my arms. I started fighting, kicking, and screaming. The men were able to pull me off the porch.

"Ouch!" he cried. I bit him, then I grabbed the pole.

"Bellina, stop acting like this," Mrs. Levine scolded, but I could not surrender. I was howling and shouting.

"Mama, mama, help me! I want my mama and papa, please, mamaaaaa, no, no, no, please. Give me back my mama!" I commanded. I was reaching for the house as they pulled me away and put me into the car. As we drove away, I turned to watch

the house fade into the distance. My
hands shook as I waved to the house. I
blew it a kiss goodbye. I didn't know when
I was going to return.

Chapter 2

The winter storm closed a lot of airlines.
The snow was not beautiful; it was the
kind you could not see through, the kind
you had to fight your way through. I sat
alone by the widow, heartbroken and tired.
The notebook and pen in my lap stared back
at me. I opened it and decided to write.

*It is me, mama. I am sorry, I did not cry
for you. I had no tears. But I miss you
more and more. I watch the doors and look
out of the window hoping this is a dream
and you and papa will come back to me. I
know you are in Heaven, but I think of God
as selfish. He could at least leave me one
of you. I miss you very much. I love you!*
Love, your Bellina

I watched the snow pass and the sky
clear during my long trip over. The people
who were sitting around me had some nice
faces, some plain faces, and some who
looked like they just preferred not to be
bothered. I saw a couple whom I wanted to
go home with. A policeman met me when I
got off the plane. He was tall, skinny,
and old, with a bushy mustache, orange,
red hair, blue eyes, and thick glasses.
   "Hello, little lady, I will be
driving you to your aunt's house. How was

your plane trip?" the man in uniform inquired. I didn't say anything.

"What's your name? Uh huh, it says here your name is Bellina."

"Yes."

"That's a start. I'm Billy. You can just consider me your personal escort. How old are you?"

"Ten," I said abruptly. I wasn't in the mood for small talk.

"You're a brave little girl, to make that long trip here, all by yourself," he said as he tried to look at my face. I did not respond and turned my head.

The city was huge. I had been in huge cities before. New York was different. It was busy, much busier than other big cities. I didn't see anyone sitting outside of a café shop, chatting with someone.

There was no one walking the streets at ease. People guarded their purses and bodies like a bank would guard their money. A lot of roads were blocked, making us wait in traffic for many hours. The whole time I thought about my aunt, I wondered if she looked anything like my mother. Mostly I thought what if she didn't like me.

She has to like me, I thought. After all, she did want me. My mother never spoke about my aunt. I thought about why there was no mention of her. There might have been sibling rivalry, causing them to stop talking to each other.

Hmmm, this is a time I wished I had a sister, then I would not be alone. We could take care of each other, the wish pondered in my mind. We left the city and went through a neighborhood of small homes. The homes looked dark on the inside. They had broken windows and chain fences. The yards had more trash in front than the trash can. I locked my side door, hoping nothing bad would happen to me.

"Please, do not live here. Please, do not live here." My heart beat fast as I held out, to find if I would be living on this street, with the houses were falling apart. The light did not seem to shine on this neighborhood. I looked over at my escort.

Billy laughed, "Ha, ha, ha don't you worry. My bite is worse than my bark." He bit a huge chuck of the air.

I turned to the window, not paying attention to him. I wondered if she had a family. I hoped my aunt was like my mother. I pictured the way she may look, an older version of my mother. Since she was older, she preferred pearls rather than diamonds. Colors wouldn't be her favorite, only solids. Most of all, I just hoped she liked me. I wiped a tear from my cheek. "I love you," I whispered, hoping my parents could hear me.

"Well, kid, we are here at your new home," Billy stated, anticipating a reaction from me. We pulled up to a white house. It had a fence around it. The sign on the fence said *Beware*.

The house looked abandoned; so did the other houses on the street.

"Never let the outside fool you. I know you are not used to this kind of living but make the best of it." His throat was shallow when he said that. The front door opened. My heart grew excited, but I tried my best not to reveal my enthusiasm. I wanted to race out of me and into her arms. That feeling quickly changed when I saw her. My Aunt Michelle Hossett was tall, skinny, and pale. She had strings of gray hair. Her eyes had deep dark rings around them. I thought Billy would give her a cane so she wouldn't fall over when she walked. She was no version of my mother. No life came from her eyes.

"Hello, or shall I say *bonjour, ma petite fille*?" She was looking at my eyes. I pulled away from her, not wanting her to touch me or breathe on me.

"You have to be careful with her. She doesn't talk much," Billy warned. "After everything that's happen to you, how could you. It's okay, though, because I like silence. I mean, really, the only bit of sound I like to hear is John Cage's 4'33." I didn't say anything.

"Why don't you come in and put your things away while I talk to Officer." She searched his shirt for a name, "Officer Wood." She opened the door. I picked up my suitcases and went in. There weren't any lights on in the house. All the smoke could have set off the alarm.

None of the windows were open. I turned around. Aunt Michelle closed the door even more as she was talking to the officer. Across the living room was an open kitchen. I went to the sink to get some water. The kitchen looked like it had not been cleaned in years.

There were dirty dishes in the sink. On the counters were empty bottles of vodka. There were more bottles than I cared to count, different shapes and sizes, from different countries. Some were not even empty. I couldn't find a cup, so I picked a small bottle that had *Belvedere* written on it. It wasn't a new bottle; a brown stain marked it underneath.

I took it to the sink to rinse it out. Small black, white, and green round circles of mold formed around the rusty sink. I turned on the faucet. "Ahh!" I yelled, once I felt the warm water splash in my face. The faucet made a funny noise, as if food was stuck in it and was trying to choke it out. I quickly turned it off.

I stood in front of the sink, with water dripping from my face. I heard small scratching noises coming from the sink. Two large roaches were sprinting around the drain. I froze as if they were going to attack me. One roach came up from the sink hole. I quickly turned on the faucet to wash them away; brown water spurted, then splashed everywhere, sending the roaches running. I turned off the faucet, hurling my arms to my chest.

"I normally drink bottled water." I jumped when I heard her voice. "You'll find them in the refrigerator." She went to sit on the couch. I stood in front of the refrigerator. I hoped it wasn't like the sink. If it was, I thought just to skip drinking the water. I slowly cracked it open, peeking halfway in. To my surprise, it looked halfway decent from the sink.

There were more empty vodka bottles, a bag of lettuce, carrots, tomatoes, cheese, ranch salad dressing, three bottles of water, and some grapes.

"I'm a vegetarian," she called from the living room. I took one bottle and closed the door quickly. "Bellina, your mother always had a thing for Italian men. Are you sure your father is Syrian?" she began the interrogation.

"You met my father?" I requested with excitement. I wanted to know if she remembered his face.

"Hummm, of course. After all, we were family. You came after my breakdown." She looked at me. "How much about me has your mother told you?"

She was investigating my mother. Maybe it was my mother's fault for not telling me about her family. Maybe it was to protect me. I didn't want to make my mother out to be a bad person. I looked at the floor. "Your mother and I had a disagreement and she left. From time to time I got a letter. One time or another, she sent me a postcard."

"My mother told me if you have a disagreement with someone you should make up with them," I said.

"Yes, but we were too stubborn to do anything about it. I was in a hospital and I wasn't allowed to contact anyone for several months. When I was able to contact people, everyone had left. Now, she's gone and you are here with me." She leaned forward to me, putting out her cigarette.

She began rubbing her thumb under her chin. "You look so much like your mother. You have your father's eyes." She observed for a moment, then looked away. She stood and drifted down the hallway. She returned with scented candles.

The smell from the candles attempted to dominate the smoke coming from my aunt's cigarettes. The smoke clouded all the junk in the room, making the room look small. There was a painting above the fireplace. The painting had tan French doors opening to a rose-colored staircase. On top of the staircase was a bottle of vodka pouring into a glass.

The glass had a face on it. The eyes were looking at the drop and the mouth was opening up as to say "woo." The painting was called "The Little Water of Life." "*Salut* to the Russians. They are the only foreign people I like," my aunt muttered.

"Where is my room? I'm tired and would like to sleep for a while," I said as I began to yawn.

"I will allow you to sleep in the room down the hall." She sounded irritated. I thought it was my being here. "When I get the check, I may give you a good room upstairs. Until then, you must earn your stay here." She sat back on the couch and lit another cigarette.

It was a cold house. I felt more comfort with Mrs. Levin than with my aunt. The room she let me stay in was small but cleaner than the living room. It had only a bed with a window beside it. Drops of water came from the corner of the ceiling.

I still had the bottle in my hands and put it on the floor so it could catch the drops. The creamy green color wall paint made me think the room could be my own little European room. I could decorate it and make it a nice French room. I imagined I was a girl being locked in a tower and I would escape out my window. Falling into a land of gardens and sweets, I laid on the bed, falling into a sweet dream.

The drip drop sounds of the leaking water woke me. I turned over with my hands shielding my heart. My mother or my father will no longer wake me. I cried, wanting them to come back to me but the door never opened and the house was silent. I stayed in bed until the evening came. I went into the living room.

Aunt Michelle was passed out on the couch, drunk from two bottles of alcohol. Her cigarette looked like it died out. I didn't know what to do. I didn't want to wake her. There must have been a mistake. Aunt Michelle's image did not resemble my mother in any way. No grace came to mind when I thought of her. I sat at the end of the couch, thinking of the big mistake everyone made. I was not supposed to be here.

My stomach started to growl. I wanted to ignore it, but I couldn't fight the urge. There was not a huge selection of food to consider. My father told me there were people out there who were less fortunate than I. If I'm with someone, don't be rude, but take small portions. If only he saw the conditions here. The safest thing in the refrigerator was the lettuce. I grabbed a handful of clean lettuce.

The way the sun shined in the kitchen window made me smile for a moment. I walked to the door. I opened the front door and went out. Down the road I saw a school bus drive by. There were kids my age on it. The bus driver saw me and waved. They looked friendly. The bus made me want to go to school. I kind of like the idea of going to an American school. I went back into the house. Aunt Michelle had awakened.

"When do I start school?" Her hand was glued to her head. She stumbled back over to the couch. "How long was I asleep? My head feels like a train ran over it. Well, don't just stand there. Put a pot of coffee on."

"When may I go to school?"

"First let us drink our coffee, then we'll talk about getting you into school."

"I'm not allowed to drink coffee."

"Well, you're with me now. And here you can do anything you like." she revealed to me as she lit another cigarette. "Here is to freedom;" Freedom, she had liberty from whatever made her like this. I stood in the kitchen not knowing what to do. I had never made coffee.

"What's wrong with you?"

"I do not know how to make coffee."

She viewed me in disbelief. "What, no coffee? Look here, girl. See how I make it?" She pulled my arm as she marched to the coffee pot. "It doesn't take a scientist to know how to make coffee." I did not respond, for the simple fact she scared me. Her coffee took a couple of minutes to make. I thought it was disgusting when she used the dirty water from the sink to make her coffee with. "The filter cleans the water before the coffee starts to make it." Within minutes she sat down with her coffee. She drank it slowly, liked she wanted to taste every sip of the flat coffee. I got up.

"Where are you going?" She looked surprised.

"I am going to wash up and get dressed," I informed her.

"Oh … well, hurry back. I don't want you lurking through my things." I left wondering how someone like this was related to me. The fact that we were related was frightening. I thought if she opened the windows and let the sunshine in, she could be a happier person. The bathroom was next to my room. It had a sink, shower, and toilet. Above the sink was a mirror.

The bathroom was nothing special. I named the bathroom *Plain Jane*.

The first time I took a shower felt like pure-steam stone hitting me. I did not want to get out. I washed the dirt off me, dancing and singing in the shower. I went into the living room and Aunt Michelle was standing at the front door. Her back was toward me. She stood there with her hand on the knob. Her head was down as she seemed to be counting.

"Aunt Michelle, when do you think I will be able to go to school? I already have paper and pencils," I pleaded with her. She did not turn to me but, went to the kitchen.

"We must leave, before the people take us away and lock us up. They will never let us go. They are not trying to protect us," she bizarrely stated.

"Aunt Michelle, did you say something?" I asked, even though I heard every word she muttered. She mumbled something else; I did not go near her.

She moved slowly and said out loud, "I need a drink!"

I slowly went back into the room. I was in there for a couple more hours when she began screaming for me to come out. "You have been in that room all day. How do you expect to get anything done? How do you expect to eat? There is no room service here. You're not at your home anymore, you are here with ME!"

She sounded as if she wanted to say something else. She threw her hands up, leaving, slamming the door behind her. I stayed in my room until I felt safe to come out. I ran to the refrigerator to grab the lettuce that was still good. I took all of it and ran back to my room. I waited for safe signs to leave the room. A safe sign would be silence from the living room.

I wanted to hurry to and from going out of the room. The longer I was out, the greater risk I had to run into her. I never knew when Aunt Michelle would have an outburst. My insides shook, my hands were sweating, and I felt as if my insides were going to jump out of my skin from the thought of running into her. I tried to keep my distance from her.

Time passed. The days were long and the nights were short. Rain came, allowing the sun to come out and shine. I stayed in the room as much as possible. There was no one to talk with. I wrote page after page to my parents. I told them how much I missed them. I hope they were missing me, too.

I refused to write about my aunt, for fear she would ruin the little happiness I felt. Mainly, I wanted the attention from my parents for myself. Most of the time, I sat alone in the house. Aunt Michelle came home, screamed, then would leave until the next morning. She would come home in a rage, slamming the front door open, yelling, "We must leave! Get away before they lock us up! Go, go, run don't let them take us. We are not wrong, please…" she was screaming uncontrollably.

She started throwing pans and bottles, screaming, "Make it stop! Help! Don't take us, please."

As soon as I heard her coming, I ran to my room. There was not a lock on my room door. I hid behind the door, using it for a shield. The door was the force to stop her from coming in. "Please protect me, please," I pleaded with myself. I prayed she wouldn't come in as she became louder and louder. I went to hide under the covers and covering my ears. I heard BOOM, BOOM, BOOM, as Aunt Michelle hit the wall with all her might. I put my hand over my heart.

"Please, please do not let her come in here," I prayed almost in a whisper. She ranted for what seemed a lifetime. All of a sudden it got quiet; too quiet. I thought it was safe to come out.

I crept out the door, trying not to make a sound. I held my breath in awe, in disbelief at what laid before me. I walked on my tip-toes; that way, I didn't step on the broken glass that was everywhere. The food in the refrigerator was thrown out onto the floor, counter. The roaches were in delight. I continued to tip-toe around.

It surprised me that the pillows were on the couch; all of them were except for one. I walked and came to a stop when I almost tripped over something. I looked down. Aunt Michelle was curled into a ball. She was holding the pillow. She was mumbling for them not to take her. She lay in a puddle of liquor.

I ran to get the phone. I didn't allow not knowing the emergency number to stop me. I knew the operator would help me. I pulled some junk up off the floor and tossed it aside, searching for the phone. Moments later, I found it. In her rage, Aunt Michelle tore the phone from the socket. I slid some of the glass out of my way to sit next to my aunt. She was wet from sweat, cold as ice, and she looked pale as a person who was sick.

I moved her wet string of gray hair from her face. She looked sicken, a sickness I had never seen before. I got a wet rag. My mother used to pat a wet rag on me when I was sick. I wanted to help my aunt, like my mother helped me. I gently placed it on my aunt's forehead. I patted the rag over her face and around her neck. She was not responding.

Death seemed to come into my mind. If she died, I didn't know where else they would send me. I suddenly felt elated at the thought I may be finally reunited with Claudia and Tom. A woman's voice sang in my ear, *this little bird has lost its wing*. She would sing it over and over again. My aunt was the bird who lost her wing. She looked so fragile, like a tiny girl in a woman's body. Wrinkles traced her face, her veins surfaced to the top of her skin.

I wrapped a blanket around her. She stayed on the floor for a few more days, until she got better. I cared for her as if she was my child. I pulled her hair from her face and washed her hands.

"It will be okay. I won't let them take us away. I won't leave your side," I reassured her.

She slept for a couple days. I tried to clean up the vomit she would spit up. It was smeared between the floor and her face. These were not happy days. She was the first person who received my care. I waited and hoped she would not die. I didn't sleep. If she died, I prepared myself for my murder admission. One of the terms that I would request would be a transfer to a prison in Geneva, rather than going to prison here. I thought maybe it would be a good thing if she died, so she wouldn't have to worry about people taking her away any longer. After she died, I would have no choice but to die next, sooner or later.

She woke up slowly. "What happened? Why am I on the floor?" She seemed stunned at her placement. I hadn't moved her from the spot I found her. Her hand hit the bottle when she tried to get up.

"Ohhh..." she moaned. A miracle woke her up. I did not face going to prison or dying anytime soon. "Help me get up," she said attempting to rise onto her knees. She fell back down. Her voice scratched my ears. She made it over to the couch.

I remained standing. "Well, don't just stand there clean that up." She threw a sponge at me. "Clean that up." She lay down and twisted her head. The sponge was dry. I went to the kitchen sink quickly and made soapy water to clean the floor with. I scrubbed the vomit off the floor. I ignored the smell. I decided to scrub the whole the floor. Every inch needed it. It did no good. I just added more nasty dirt to the nasty dirty floor. One of the table legs in the dining room was held up by three books.

My father would have had a heart attack if he saw this. The Bible held the books down along with the half-leg of the table. *Proof* was second and *Understanding the Human Sexuality* was the third. I looked at the books. I'd only read a little of the Bible. My father thought it

was a great book. He read me the story of
Ruth; she was a heroine with great beauty.
I played her many times in my dreams.
Every night I tried to dream, to erase the
nightmare of me living here. This
nightmare was killing my spirit. It left
me here to rot.

A sour woman, my aunt soaked in her
own misery. She had nothing to teach me,
she seemed to know less than I did. I felt
sorry for her, along with myself. She fell
asleep again. I wanted to wake her so her
last words were not *clean that up*. Looking
at her, told me she didn't know of
anything else to say. It was probably best
she died, saying that.

If she was awakened unexpectedly, she
may utter something much worse. I had
whole-heartedly decided to clean the house
as she lay asleep. Here and there as I
tip-toed around her, checking to see if
she was alright, the books holding the
table steady caught my attention. I
flirted with them dally.

"Hello. Would you like to be read? I
see so. I also see you are not having as
much fun being a leg supporter. One day,
friends, I'll save you gracefully." They
made me want to go back to school. I sat
beside them and dreamt what the pages
read.

Proof appeared to be about a boy on a
journey to Egypt to unlock an ancient
king's tomb. I was sure it had to be
filled with war, love, mystery, and deep

secrets. The book was thick; it must have sat there collecting dust for ages. There were no pictures inside the book.

It made me only want to read it more. I figured the language must have been romantically written for it not to show scenery. From time to time I scoped around to see if my aunt had awoken. For the short moments, I loved it when she slept. The quietness left me forgetting what the purpose of the books was actually for. I continue to read the titles of the other two books, hoping Aunt Michelle didn't wake to my cries. The book underneath the Bible and *Proof* was, *Understanding the Human Sexuality.*

The sun went down and the crickets came out. I liked the sound of the crickets. The sounds were pleasant. They were much more pleasant than the sounds I recently had grown accustomed to hearing. I sat by the books, admiring the sounds of the crickets. My only wish was to see them.

I closed my eyes watching the crickets transform from dull unwanted insects to song singing, colorful printed sites of joy. That's the wonderful part about dreaming; the ugly turns to beauty and the bad turns to great. It's more than an escape; it's the dream that one day I will be able to escape and my life would be nice.

Chapter 3

When I woke, Aunt Michelle was nowhere to
be found. She had left a note to clean the
whole house. The house was a mess and
smelled of vomit, cigarettes, and old
beer. It was a mess four days after she
made me scrub it from top to bottom. My
hands were cracked and bleeding. I washed
them slowly so I wouldn't hurt too badly
from the sting of the water.

The smile on my aunt's drunken face
made my face tense beyond anger. I bit my
lower lip to keep myself from crying. She
saw a poor girl dressed in a dingy tee
shirt, using her side feet for balance
because the rest of her feet were covered
in blisters. I felt hopeless as I was
laughed at. Every day became the same
cycle; she would leave for several days,
returning to wreck the house for me to
clean it.

The house smelled of never finding
vomit and smoke. My stomach turned upside
down, aching with the most straining pain.
It left me feeling weak and dizzy. I had
never felt like this before. The taste
left in my mouth forced its way up,
bursting out of me too fast for me to ever
make it to the toilet. I could do nothing
but lie on the cold floor, next to the
thick, nasty smelling liquid. I tried to
fight keeping my eyes open. The more and

more I did, the heavier they became until I gave up.

In my dreams a white horse rescued me. The beautiful white horse kissed me, giving me strength. It picked me up off the floor and we galloped away to a beautiful garden. My father and mother stood in the center of the garden, waiting for me. I ran into their arms, feeling their warmth and smelling how lovely their scents were. We cried because we were happy; happy to be together.

My eyes opened to reality that I was not in their arms, and the scent I smelled was vomit. I had no choice but to clean, afraid of what my punishment would be if I didn't. I began with the bathroom. Not finding any mops or sponges to clean with, I took the rag in the bathtub. I hand washed and squeezed it dry. Then I got on my hands and knees to clean the floor.

Several times I had to put my nose under my shirt to protect myself from the smell, only to pull my nose back out because my shirt smelt just as bad. The faster I cleaned the place, the less I smelled it. Being alone gave me more chances to sing out loud all the poems in my head. I sung as loud as I could, until my lungs hurt.

"*I was once alone on a ship*
A ship that sail on the black sea
An old ship I grown to love

Angry winds, crying rain came and
blew my old ship out the way
My old ship, my old ship
My old ship was thrown out the way."

The song made me work fast,
forgetting about the smell. It made me
forget about the pain from the blisters
popping on my feet as I walked. Before I
knew it, I was done with the bathroom. I
went into the kitchen. Bottles and trash
lay everywhere. A few dishes were on the
counter.

I threw the bottles into the trash.
Some of the bottles wouldn't fit. I set
them in the corner of the counter. I
continued to clean the kitchen, then I
moved on to the living room. I had to
scrub the couch and the rug. I scrubbed so
hard my arms started to ache.

The living room could not be helped.
It was time to move to clean the hallway.
The hallway floor was a mess because of
me. My footprints stained the floor. I had
to get on my knees to clean the floor,
first by picking up my dead skin from my
blisters that rubbed off when I walked.
The dead skin had dried up quickly.

There were all sizes, big and little.
Some of the dead skin was stuck in between
the floor and the dried water caused from
my blisters. Once I picked up my dead
skin, I went back and washed the floor. My
knees were rubbing and thinning as I slid
them up and down on the floor. I dared not

look at the bottom of my feet. I was
scared of what I might see.

I continued to scrub until I couldn't
do it anymore. At the end of the hallway,
I stopped to take a break. I had lost my
breath and my throat was dry, I sat there
not wanting to move. After sitting for
what seemed like hours, I picked myself up
and made my way to the kitchen. I grabbed
the last bottle of water and gulped every
last bit of it.

I tried to be careful that the water
made it into my mouth and not onto the
floor. I drank it with the shakes and
jitters. I drank it like I was a dying man
finding water for the first time in a long
time. It was like I had no control. It was
like I could not taste or feel the water
going down in me. It was like the reaction
Aunt Michelle had when she drunk her
vodka. The body automatic needs it.
Without it, your body goes on a search
until it has it. I could not stop shaking,
losing all control of my body.

The house was so silent my ears made
their own music. The music made my head
spin. I shook my head to make it stop. I
preferred the silence over the music. I
would have done anything for it. It wasn't
long before the music stopped playing.

The day had been dreadful. I looked
to find anything to keep my mind at ease.
The only thing I could focus on was the
stairs. Aunt Michelle said nothing about
going upstairs. I wondered to whom the

rooms belonged to upstairs. The staircase
was tempting, I fell the staircase calling
for me, as if it had a secret to tell me.
I walked from it, for the fear of my aunt
coming home. If she caught me upstairs
there was no telling how she would react
or what she would do to me. So, I stayed
downstairs for safety.

I finished cleaning the house. The
smell was almost gone. Part of me knew
that a bit would always linger. I had been
wearing the same clothes since I arrived.
Not once had my aunt washed any underwear
for me. I wasn't sure if it was me or the
house that carried the awful odor.

It made no sense to take a shower and
get back into dirty clothes. My mother had
taught me how to hand wash my clothes. She
and Claudia had to wash their own clothes
when they were in Kenya. I just needed
some soap. I was out of the bar of soap my
aunt gave me. I asked her for another and
she turned and said, "Pas Chance." From
then on I stood in the shower to let the
water rinse me. Hot water hit my back and
poured down my body. The steam came from
the heat the water gave off. I had slowly
rotated around to get all the parts of my
body. It was the day's Aunt Michelle was
not here that I could take a long shower.
I would put back on my dirty clothes. I
thought it was alright because I was still
dirty.

"Aunt Michelle, are you home? Hello?"
I called to her from the toilet. I knew it

was silly to yell, but I had no choice. I was out of toilet paper. I sat on the toilet for a couple minutes, figuring out what to do. It didn't take long for me to pick my head up and stare directly to the answer. First, I wiggled and squeezed my stomach to try to drain all the pee and poop I had left out of me. Once I thought all of it was out, I got up and crossed my legs to make sure no leftovers dripped out of me. I flushed the toilet and duck walked to turn on the shower. It splashed out. I crouched down while turning the faucet to the perfect setting for me. I jumped into the shower and whipped the tub side from any droppings from me. I was in the shower cleaning away all the waste with my hand. When I was finished I got out and completely dried off. Along with the soap I couldn't find any toilet paper. I took four showers that day.

It had hit me that some soap and toilet paper may be upstairs in the bathroom she used.

I wanted to go upstairs to the bathroom. I figured she wouldn't be home until the end of the week and, without thinking, I went. I reached the top of the stairs. There were three doors, two facing each other and one at the end. I did not see why one person lived in a big house. I hesitated, walking to one of the doors. I wanted to turn around to go downstairs. I was already up. My nerves felt like a thin

tread being pulled down upon by heavy
liquid.

It was not a comfortable feeling; it
held me back. The doors moved into the
others' spot. They moved fast as my eyes
tried to catch up with them. My head felt
heavy, as did my eyes. I thought I was
going to collapse. I grabbed the staircase
to slowly sit myself down. I waited until
I felt strong enough to get up. I needed
the soap. The only way to get the soap was
to go get it. The door on the left I
opened first. My heart skipped a beat, my
mouth opened. No words came out. Shock
overcame me.

A little boy lived here, in the small
perfect room. The bed had not been made
and there were toys on the floor. There
were no pictures in sight. A black and
white photo of a girl on her tip-toes
dressed in a woman's dress kissing the
cheek of a boy dressed in a man's suit
holding a briefcase, outside a small house
with a puppy running around them hung on
the blue wall.

There was a toy train next to puzzle
pieces beside the bed. The closet door was
slightly open. The room looked sad, as if
it was waiting for the little boy to come
back. My mind told me to find the soap.
But I felt like the boy's room wanted me
to stay. I closed it behind me and went
on, hoping to find the bathroom. I had a
feeling the door across the room was not
the bathroom. I did not have to go in to

be sure of it. I rested my head on the door, deciding to leave it closed.

The bathroom was plain as all the other rooms. A painting of a woman looking over her shoulder, baring her back, hung on the wall. She had a seductive look on her face. Her hair was curled. She wrapped herself in a lime green veil. She floated through the rue of a European village. *Bienvenue* read on the doors. On the rue were fruits and flowers to grace her. The portrait was beautiful. At the bottom it signed *Lucien Heux*. He had got every angle, every curve correct.

I had forgotten all about the soap. The art had my attention. When I looked at it more clearly, the painting was my mother. It was her. My mother was the woman in the painting. She looked right at me. She had been stored in the painting. I sat on the toilet lid. She looked like an Egyptian queen. I closed the door, so it was just me and her.

Aunt Michelle came back home on a Saturday. She was in no mood for anything. She allowed me to go outside, only to sit on the front steps. The day was nice. The rain had left the sky fresh. I felt chills on my back; fall was coming. I wrote in the dirt. "In fall I miss you the most." I wished they were with me. Going to work is what led up to parents death.

Everyone who goes to work is in danger. I came to that conclusion. It's a trade-off. If I go to work, I put myself

in danger of being killed. If I stay home,
I put myself in danger of not surviving. I
must accept death, I know that. Only do I
go to it or have it come to me. They were
not supposed to go "too soon, too soon."
Tears fell from my eyes. I put my hand
over my heart as I started to cry. I felt
pain, the type of pain that was not ready
to leave you. She came to sit with me for
a while. We could not remember the good
things, just the part that was missing.

I was all cried out when I saw the
school bus. It drove by, no students were
on. "Where would it go on a Saturday?" I
thought out loud. A bird flew by, came
back, circled and whistled. It then flew
away. It was a sign. I was thirteen. I had
been out of school for two years now. The
house behind me had become my jail.

One evening, a few candles lit the
house. My aunt had mostly stayed in her
room. She came down to get a glass of
water. I stood close to her not thinking I
could ask. My throat became dry. Under my
nails moist had sat. My foot shook to an
unsteady beat. I hesitated to look at my
aunt. She was on her way back to her room.
"I want to go to school!" words blurted
out of my mouth. It wasn't me saying these
words out loud.

"You go to school," she mocked back.
The idea made her laugh. "Listen girl, you
will go to school when I tell you you can
go!"

"When will that be?" She did not like my question.

"This is your life now! Ain't no need to change it. Hell, most of the kids in school wish they were not and the few who like being there are the smart ones!"

"But I'm smart, too!" My voice rose from my throat.

"You sound like your mother. I'm smart too." she laughed as she mocked my mother and me. "She was supposed to be smart, too," She looked around the room. She turned around on the stairs. My eyes begged her to take me to school. "Look at you. You have nothing to wear. No money to buy school things. You talk back. You are dirty. American schools do not like dirty immigrants." She ran downstairs, rushing at me. My hands flew up in defense as she grabbed my arm, took her cigarette, and plugged it into my arm.

If one were to ask me if I had ever felt the burning of fire, I would say yes. It sticks to you while it eats away your skin. It makes your eyes want to pop out of your head. It leaves you screaming for death. It hurts.

"Here, this will settle that brain of yours." She splashed her glass of water over me. It claimed the pain from the fire of the cigarette on my arm. But I still hurt. I kept my arms up in protest from her grip but quickly settled down. I just thought if she saw how obedient I was, she would allow me to go to school. But the pain was so severe; I felt my head explode as I bit skin off my lips and licked the blood. Her hands still held my arms tight. I opened my eyes after being shaken to her finger pointing at me. "If you want to go to school, then so be it. You will not receive any help from me. And I guarantee you this; you will be the dumbest kid there." She then threw me back onto the coffee table and ran upstairs, slamming the door. My body was numb. My heart was racing. She didn't tell me yes or no. It was up to me.

With success there is a cost, sometimes even pain. I was crying because I was happy with what I got. I got the option to go, deciding to go tomorrow. Getting ready was a challenge. Aunt Michelle still hadn't noticed the bar of soap missing in her bathroom. A good thing for me when she went to sleep, I washed my clothes. They didn't come out very well, instead of only being wet, they smelt of bad odor. I decided not to go. I sat on the edge of my bed, feeling lost. I watched the day go by from my window. Soon night came.

"You can't just focus on going to school all day. The housework has to be done, too." My aunt stopped me before I went to bed. Her voice was dry and harsh. She handed me a list of chores to do. It was long, beginning with clean the bathroom, clean the kitchen, mop the floor, vacuum the floor dust the furniture... I cleaned while she sat and watched television. She ate chips and fish and told me not to even ask for any and I could have an egg with milk and toast.

I took what she gave me and went to bed. The sun shined, I sat up, thinking today would be the day. I stood, looking down at my bruised feet. I knew today wouldn't be the day. I was in the house alone, so I went to sit outside. I had the urge to run away, but I had nowhere to run to. The only satisfaction would be of knowing my aunt wouldn't come looking for me.

I spent most days on the step watching the ants chase one another. I breathed a lot outside. The fresh air made its way into my lungs, making me feel a little better. Before dark, I went inside to my room. My aunt was scrambling around, getting ready to leave; she slammed the front door behind her. I tip- toed out of bed, to peek out the door.

The house was dark; the only light came from the moon and the cigarette she left burning beside an open bottle of Grey Goose. A breeze whistled outside. It shook the leaves of the trees. The creepy sound of someone tapping on the window made me jump. The lights flickered on and off. A storm couldn't have caused it; there was no sign in sight. Rain did not drop. The wind sounded as if it was trying to get into the house.

I sat on the corner of the couch. She did not come home that night. The night became still. I went to bed with letters on my mind. During the lunch breaks in school, my friends and I would write each other letters. When it was time for us to go back to class we would hand them out. One of the letters Juliet gave me had left me in a good mood for the rest of the week.

Bellina,
Je vous aime pour mon ami. Ayez un beau jour.
Juliet.

It was simple and nice. I love it. I kept it in my pocket. On the days when I was down I put my hand over my pocket and took a deep breath then let go. The letters I wrote said
Ayez un beau jour.
That is what everyone wrote. But her letter to me said
Je vous aime mon ami. Ayez un beau jour.
During class I would look at her. She caught my eye and waved back to me. We never got to really become friends; that following month I had to leave. The letters, Juliet, and the school were just memories now. I fell asleep with those memories.
The morning sky woke me to the sun shining over my face. I had felt like I

was drugged as I lay in bed. My eyes
opened and closed. My focus was caught in
a net of getting up, staying in bed,
eating… Wednesday was the day, I thought.
I felt chained to my bed. For a moment I
forgot where I was.

The soundless house put a whistle in
my ears. If a feather hit the floor, I
could hear it. She wasn't home. I felt the
freedom to pick up and leave my room
without a peek to find where she was. I
ran to sit on the couch.

"OUCH!" I screamed, jumping up. The
wire in the couch poked my butt and
stabbed me in the back. It was an
uncomfortable, painful ache. I imagined
the bruise it left on my butt and back. I
didn't want to make it worse, so I lay on
my stomach on the floor. The rain came
down, steadily putting me to sleep. When I
slept, I dreamed of my mother. Her voice
told me everything will be alright.

The music came on, blasting
throughout the whole house. I looked out
the window, expecting to see people in the
streets having a great time, but there
were no one. The music played and I danced
to it. I threw my arms into the air, moved
my hips, twirled, and kicked my legs out.

I moved to the music. Her voice gave
attitude; so did my movement. I fell on my
knees exhausted, but her music still kept
playing. I never heard this type of music
before. It was better than my aunt's
silent sympathy. She sung and I moved.

I was out of breath and loved every minute of it. She had stopped playing the music. I felt my life stop as I caught my breath. Minutes seem like hours before the music started again. It was low, and then grew into a loud blast. I let my hair fly, my feet tap; I had the best time. The music wasn't graceful. I tried to make my moves graceful, but the music wouldn't allow me.

It was wild I had no choice but to be wild. I kept thinking this was the sound my parents danced to, because my father was to hyper to have danced slowly. I pictured him dragging my mother off the floor and swinging her around, shouting, "Go ahead. Move like this!" She had moved like this, laughing throughout the entire song. Before my time in existence, I was my parents' friendly ghost.

I was there as they danced, watching in a distance as their faces lit the room. I knew they were going to be together past their days. Their together now and it's time for them to be my friendly ghost as I move like this, and moved I did. I wanted to be on the outside. Prison walls caved on me until I couldn't breathe. It was until I was outside that all the weight in the world raised from my chest. Pound, Release, Pound, Release; I just breathed slowly.

Not allowing my thoughts to stand in my way, I breathed slowly all the way across the street, to the house where the music came from. My heart was following the music. I went in the open door and sat down. My head felt like a feather. I don't remember anything after that, only waking up to her.

"I made an apple brie and meat loaf with fresh greens and carrots. For some reason Northerners don't care for Southern food. I figure since I moved here, I'll try something different. I should adapt to just about all the changes here. I just threw my hands up and said, Lord if this is what you want me to adapt to, and then help me do it in your ways." She took a moment to look around her house.

I had no idea how long I had been sleeping. I laid my head back down on the pillow. There was no sun in the sky. My stomach growled. "Oh, that poor stomach of yours; here, baby, let me get you a plate. Your parents must be worried sick. You must be new to our neighborhood because I've never seen you around. I'm Ms. Hickens. You can call me Ruth."

I looked at her. Her skin was brown and looked smooth. She had beautiful big brown eyes, with a kind smile that made her cheeks plump up. She looked like a caretaker with plenty of food to feed many children. "Like the woman in the Bible, Ruth?" I asked, but she looked like she could be much more than Ruth. She looked like a mother.

Ruth's parents must have thought she was going to be real special to name her after a woman in the Bible. "Yes, there's a woman in the Bible named Ruth, but my parents just like the name. And what's your name?"

"Bellina," I answered.

"I like that; it's different. Now eat this, child. It's something new I whipped up. You look like you haven't eaten in years." She stared in silence, then she softly said, "New York isn't a place for young girls to wander into someone's place like you do. Eat so you can hurry home and tomorrow you can come back with your parents' permission. Slow down, child. There is plenty of food."

"This is good. Thank you!" Every bite was delicious. I wanted to stay on her couch the whole night. It was the kind of couch that soaked you into it. The wine red couch had tan cream throw pillows on it. Tall plants stood in the corners.

An Indian rug of gold with red roses decorated the floors in the house. A coco cherry wood coffee table was the center of attention in the living room. Photos of exotic lands hung on the walls. The food carried the smell of rich spices throughout the house. The lights dimmed enough to make the house look as if I was in a mini bistro. "I got those photos from a friend of mine. He's a pastor in Kenya. Kenya is in Africa. Have you ever heard of it?"

"I have," I said with a mouth full of food. "I do not feel like talking anymore.

May we eat in silence?" She slowly traced
me with her eyes, then nodded in
agreement. The truth be told, I wanted to
hear more about Kenya and other exotic
lands she knew but I couldn't believe I
made it out of my aunt's house. I didn't
want to talk to her because of the tears
that would start to come. My food couldn't
get spoiled from my tears. I was too
hungry. She ate in silence and, when my
plate was almost finished, she got me
more. I ate three platefuls.

"Now that you finish, it is better
you make it home before it is too late,"
she told me. I wanted to scream *help me,
let me stay with you, I will be good, I
promise*. The heartbreak of being turned
away made me leave. Mrs. Hickens shouted
at me, "Look both ways before you cross
the street." I turned back around and
waved her off. Then I turned and walked
without looking across the street. Ms.
Hickens was just like everyone else, I
thought. With all of my force I slammed
the door shut. Aunt Michelle screamed at
me, "Re-shut the door, this time with
common sense."

I jumped when I heard her loud,
demanding voice. She could scare anyone. I
quietly opened and shut the door. My feet
twisted back toward her to stand in a
frozen state. My hands folded into one
another. The tighter I held them, the
faster I could stop shaking. The grip that
had locked my hands together made me feel

secure for a second. That was until I
looked at my aunt's eyes. All security
left, leaving my heart to beat a little
faster by the second. The lights were off
in the house. Only a candlelight lit part
of the table Aunt Michelle sat at.

"Where have you been all day?"

I became cold as I wondered for
answers. "Well, did you go out and come
back deaf? I asked you a question. I
better hear an answer within the next
minute!" She pulled out a cord and placed
it on the table in my view. My feet
tinkled from the warm liquid that ran down
my leg.

"I went out for a bit." My voice
trembled as my body shook uncontrollably.

"For what?" she demanded.

"I, I, I went to see if the school
bus came any other of the times or day."

"And what did you found out?"

"I didn't find out anything."

"Come sit down across from me."

I didn't bother to step over the
urine on the floor. I kept hands folded in
front of me. I ignored how cold I was as I
sat in my urine on the hard wood chair.

We sat for a minute in silence, long
enough for my feet to become numb and the
urine to dry.

"I have decided not to use this cord
on you. I am not that much of a monster,
like you think I am," She softly said.

My feet started to itch. I wiggled
them to stop the stinging. My aunt did not

want to be known as a monster. I thought
maybe she did have feelings; just not for
me. At one point, I picked my head up and
looked at her through a different angle.
Her face had softened; she caught me
looking at her and turned with harshness
in her eyes. Monster or not, she still
hurt me, and I did not know what to do, if
I could do anything at all.

Chapter 4

During the time my aunt left me, I escaped
across the street to Ms. Hickens' home. I
loved how her home always smelled of
spices. Most of all, I loved how she
always had time for me. She made me feel
special, something I hadn't felt since the
death of my mother. I knew my mother would
not mind if I loved Ms. Hickens. At her
house, I felt right at home. I noticed the
travel books on her coffee table. They
were of exotic places, like Morocco,
Egypt, and other distant lands.

    "Ms. Hickens?" I said.

    "Yes?" she replied.

    "Have you been to these places?" I
asked her.

    "I've been to Morocco. I went there
last fall; it was beautiful." She took a
seat next to me. The books were next to a
stunning ivory and gold globe. The color
of the countries on the globe was in dark
colors of red, green, orange, and browns.
I wanted to touch the globe, but I was
nervous because it looked very elegant to
touch. Ms. Hickens reached for it and spun
the globe making the color shine with
radiance as it spun around in its royal
colors.

    "The world holds endless
possibilities of the places you can be,"

Ms. Hickens informed me, spinning the globe.

"I know I can go anywhere in the world," I told her.

"A lot of people know they can go anywhere." Ms. Hickens leaned over to me. "A lot of them forget that, when they are put into situations they cannot control."

"I won't forget that. Not ever." It was true. I had never forgot; I could go anywhere in the world. Even living in my aunt's dark and lonely house, I knew I could go anywhere because my mother and father took me places and talked about the places I had yet to see.

"And I will help you never forget that," Ms. Hickens assured me. "I found this globe in a dumpster around the corner. It kills me when people throw useful things away. All I did was wipe, shine and it looks brand new. Pick a place you want to go to, anywhere in the world."

"I want to know more about Morocco." I was certain of my choice.

"Ah, Morocco is where your plane landed." Ms. Hickens opened the book on the table.

"My plane?" I repeated, revealing my yellow teeth. I was excited to escape my dark world, "Let's go!"

She decorated the house in bright colors. Large blank canvas lay on the floor with paint of all colors in cans. All the furniture had been moved. Rugs with throw pillows that made a circle took

the furniture's place. The kitchen was off
limits but I could still smell the rice
steaming, the lamb baking in the oven
releasing the species in the air. The
kitchen transformed into a small bistro in
Casablanca. Arabian tones played
throughout the bistro.

"We have to get to the bistro from
the airport," I reminded her.

"What would be our transportation?"

"Let's take a camel." I grabbed the
chair, pulling it to the middle of the
living room, following with another. Ms.
Hickens threw a sheet over the chairs.
"Let's go!" We climbed onto our camel.
"Off we go!" I saluted my hand in the air.
We traveled on our camels, trailing on the
desert sands. The fresh air made me feel
as if I floated on a cloud as cars raced
pass me, honking their horns. My camel
took her time, allowing me to feel, the
sunrays on my skin, making me feel like I
was free from the dark world I have known
for a while. But at this moment, I had
never known that dark world, only the
world where the sun shined all day.

"Before you sit, put this on." Ms.
Hickens gave me a red dress with a red
veil to keep.

"That smells good," I said as we sat
on the throw pillows and ate the lamb and
rice. When the food was gone and the
laughing stopped, I blurted out the
thoughts I had lingering in me, "Ms.
Hickens, may I ask you a question?"

"Of, course you may, baby." She looked at me with her big brown eyes.

"Why are you so nice to me?" I asked her.

"It is okay for you to ask me that. I have been kind of waiting for you or me to say something." She folded her napkin with her hands. "When I found you sleeping on my couch, I saw your bruises. You looked like whoever has been beating you also has not fed you, and you looked so safe sleeping when I saw you." She then looked away. "I know what it's like, sugar. I was beat when I was your age and you remind me of me. I just wanted you to be safe," she said.

I was speechless. I thought my mother and father had brought us together. "Thank you," I said.

"Bellina, I want you to know, it is not okay. You do not deserve to be hit," she told me with the gentlest eyes. I wanted to stay forever, but I was scared to ask, for fear of being rejected.

"I must go." I got up. "May I come back?" I knew the answer.

"Anytime, if you need anything, I mean anything, just ask." She walked me to the door. I turned around and hugged her. She knew what it was like to live in a dark world, making me feel close to her.

I always left the front door unlocked so I could come back in, but I stopped as soon as I heard her cold, demanding voice. "Come here." She was sitting toward the front door. I sat across the table from her trying to avoid looking at her careless eyes. There was a half-empty bottle next to her hand. Before tonight would be over, I knew my aunt would be finishing a couple more bottles. I waited for her to hit me or scream, but she just sat starring and she fell asleep. So, I went to the room and stayed there until it was safe to come out.

I expected her house to be back to normal with no signs of Casablanca every existing.

"I've been waiting for you." I was wrong. Casablanca stayed and survived my absences.

"Thank you for waiting for me. I am ready to go back to Casablanca."

"Go back? We are already there!" I smiled at the books on the floor. All were about Morocco and Africa. Ms. Hickens went into the kitchen and brought out a plate of Tunisian tajine and green tea that had a leaf floating in it.

"It's my own recipe, a twist on an Italian frittata. I think you should try every different kind of tea on our travels." She looked at me with concern in her voice. "What's wrong?" She was my only friend.

"Nothing, I am happy to be here," I told her.

"I'm happy you are here, too. Now let's have some fun." She guided me in to where our bistro was and placed a blank canvas in front of me. "I thought it would be fun if you painted Morocco."

"You want me to paint all of Morocco?"

"You could or you could paint the places we visit."

The trays of paint were in front of me. My eyes saw an exciting movement of vibrating shadows that danced to the tones being played. My painting wasn't the best, it wasn't the prettiest, but it sure was nice.

"Wow that is beautiful. I think you capture the heart of Casablanca."

"Thank you. What is next on our trip?"

"We are going to put these up. Hand me those pins there, please." She started pinning my paintings on the wall, "Then we're going to pop some popcorn and watch our movie."

"I knew that would make you smile."

I pretended to be in a theater, with my popcorn in one hand and my ticket in the other. The lights were dim, the movie started, I leaned back in my seat with a huge smile, happy to be there. Soon the sunset started to set. Ms. Hickens wrapped me a plate of food and Tunisian tajine to go. I had enough food to last a week.

"Well, the next time we will pick a new place to travel to. Anywhere in the world you want to go."

"I would like that." I was standing by the door with my plate and outfit in my hand.

"Be careful going home."

I was careful not to drop my food, walking home. I turned the knob, pushing in the door, but it was locked. I tried again, and the door did not open. So, I went to the back door and tried to open, it but it was locked, too. The only thing I could think of was my aunt was home.

I couldn't knock on the door and have her open it. She would have taken my food and clothes, then beat me until I told her where I had been. I walked around. The corner of my eye caught one of the windows being slightly open. I was tall enough to climb into it.

The window laid into the kitchen. I climbed into the sink and looked around. She wasn't home. I jumped down from the sink to the front door. I ran out and around to get my stuff and back to the front door. I reached to open the door, running straight into it. It was locked. Someone was in the house.

I looked back across the street to Ms. Hickens' house. I knew if I went back there, my aunt would beat me, even more severely when I came back. I decided to try the window again. I had balanced my plate and my outfit on the surface of the window. Both my hands carefully pulled my body up so my things wouldn't fall.

I picked my head to catch my breath before I pulled the rest of my body through the window. My plate of food and my outfit was snatched from the window. I lost my balance and fell onto the ground. The window slammed shut. I looked up to my aunt staring down at me. She had an angry expression on her pale face.

Raindrops dropped like tears, one at a time around me. The sun disappeared below as my aunt turned to leave me outside. I grabbed a pile of dirt to hold back my tears. I let go when the rain came pouring down. My tears blended in with the rain. Within seconds my clothes were soaked. I did not see any form of shelter. I walked to the front of the house. I started banging on the door.

"Please, please, let me in. Please!" I shouted as loud as I could. The higher my pitch, the higher the thunder roared. I stopped and turned around, ready to run across the street and stay with Ms. Hickens, but as soon as my foot was in front of the other, Aunt Michelle opened the door and yelled at me to get inside.

"Clean up this mess you flooded my floor with. How stupid are you, girl!" Her hand sent a shock wave across my face. She grabbed my shoulders and shook me to make me lose my balance and fall to the floor. I saw the rage in her eyes as her hand went up. My arms quickly protected my face as she used all her force to beat me. My mind took me back to the bistro Ms.

Hickens and I spent the day at. Aunt
Michelle got up and threw a bottle at the
door.

"What is the sound of all that God
damn noise?" She ran to the table and
picked up the bottles. The house was
scattered with other empty and half full
bottles. Every time the thunder roared she
would throw a bottle at the door cursing
in the Lord's name.

I stayed on the floor, not
understanding what she was saying. I was
fearful that her mind was full of alcohol.
The poison ripped through every vein in
her body. Now the toxins made their way to
her brain. I made my way to the room,
vowing to never drink, so I would never
become like my aunt. I didn't sleep until
I knew my aunt went to sleep. Even then I
wasn't completely asleep. The morning
came; she was shaking in her sweat.

She mumbled a few words, but I
thought to let her be. I went into the
bathroom, turned the shower head on, and
stood there. A chair was by the toilet. I
moved the chair under the door knob. Then
I locked the door.

In this moment I was safe enough to
take a shower. With the soap in my hand my
body was curled in a ball at the far end
of the tub. The water just poured down
from the shower head. The thought of the
water touching my skin, made my heart race
as I hid my face in my hands. My body

slowly started to rock itself back and forth.

The shower still poured with the soap in my hand. My hands formed a bowl for the water to pour in. I tossed the water over me. More and more I tossed the water from my hand over my body. I washed myself, sitting at the corner of the tub. I didn't want the beating from the shower hitting my body. The clean towels hung on a plastic hanger. They weren't the soft, warm, fluffy kind anyone could hug and cuddle.

They were just regular white towels, the kind a rich woman's maid would use to dry her pearl white poodle. I removed the chair and unlocked the door. I found a nice pair of jeans and tee shirt from the bag of clothes Aunt Michelle gave me. My newly washed hair was still dripping.

Normally I would air dry my hair, but I didn't want to get sick. As I was drying my hair, my aunt appeared in the doorway of my room. She had looked sick. Her eyes wouldn't stay up. Her hands shook. The tear that was trying to keep still finally rolled down. Two more followed. She then turned around and simply left. The door never closed so quietly.

I decided not to go to Ms. Hickens that day. I didn't run to the window to see which way my aunt went. I stayed in the room to avoid smelling the piles of dried vomit. The five years I have been here the smell of the house never seemed to go away. I came out of the room and noticed Aunt Michelle's door was open. I went up the stairs to my aunt's room. The room, to my amazement, didn't look like it belonged to my aunt.

There were no bottles or cigarettes. No dirt in sight. Candles on the dresser were burned out. A framed picture of a young man and woman was on a nightstand next to the bed. The notation under the picture read, "Our love will sustain through the fires that life throws our way. Take this and show us as a testament of how endless love can be."

They were in love with each other. I had read once that two people who are in love will show the same facial features in their lifetime. My aunt looked beautiful and full of life. I stared at the picture, unable to pinpoint why my aunt and I looked so much alike. I looked more like my aunt than my mother; we had the same chin and smile.

I took the picture to the mirror on the wall. My eyes did not look like my father's eyes. I looked at the young man in the picture, then I put it down. I flavored my aunt more than my mother, in the picture. The young man held his hand, covering my aunt's stomach.

She was pregnant and they were happy. The dresser the photo was on had a lock on it. The lock made me curious about what was inside. Something so secretive had to be locked away from the world to discover.

I looked at the open door; the way she lived downstairs did not tell who my aunt was. The dresser that held her secret was the aunt I wanted to know.

I wanted to know the woman in the picture, who lived, loved, and had someone, who loved her back. I left her room exactly the way it was. I waited for her at the door. I stood for a long time. She never came. I stepped back and began counting out loud.

If the door didn't twist open, I started over at 200 and counted my way back to one. It was when I finished counting from a thousand to one. I realized she was not coming back. Her body left on a search.

The sun hit me with its heat when I opened the door. The heat felt so good, I stepped all the way out. I sat on the steps. I danced a little, hopping around in front of the door. A school bus stopped down the street, kids got off. I wanted to go and meet them, but I was dirty. I wasn't the girl with the new clothes and the curly hair. I was wearing the same clothes for weeks. I saw a couple kids walking toward me. I ran back into the house. My heart was pounding on the door. Please, I hope they didn't see me. I was ashamed.

I stood outside Mrs. Hickens' door the following day. I had hope that even with my badly bruised face she'd accept me in her home. I knocked twice and there she stood. Her expression changed from joy to shock then disgust, within less than a second. I could only bite my lower lip, looking down, hoping she didn't mind how I look.

"Come in, baby." She led me in with a deep, soft tone that sounded like she was hurt. We sat on the couch, not knowing what to do or say. I've had worse bruises than this, those she had never seen. "I know we don't know one another well, but you can stay with me if you like." She covered my hand with her hand; I covered hers with mine.

"I would like that very much," I told her and stay I did. I took her son's room. She settled me in her son's room. He had a bed table in front of his bed. All his clothes were hung in the closet. There weren't any dressers; a small library of books was next to the clothes. Ms. Hickens fluffed the pillows for me.

"These pillows have not had a human's head touch them in such a long time. I can't believe how long it's been."

"How long has it been?" I asked.

"A long time." She brought out a picture of her son. "We had a disagreement and he left and never came back. He writes me a letter every now and again about how my grandchildren are doing." She sat next to me on the bed. She was still holding the picture.

"I write letters to my parents
sometimes." I wanted her to know I
understood the feeling of lost.

"That always helps," Ms. Hickens said
smiling. "It's time you get some sleep.
Tomorrow we will catch a plane first thing
in the morning to Argentina."

She tucked me in the bed. I waited
for her to get by the door.

"Good night. I love you." We looked
at each other. I smiled at her. She
returned the smile.

"I love, you, too, baby. Good night
and have sweet dreams."

I woke snuggle in blankets, on clean
sheets. I pressed my head deeper on the
pillow, pulling the blankets closer to me.
I hadn't slept so well in a long time; I
did not want to get up. I wasn't afraid; I
was safe, I would never return to my aunt
again. "How did you sleep?" Ms. Hickens
asked me, once I made it out of the room
and into the kitchen.

"Very well," I answered. "What are we
going to do today?"

"How about we eat then play a game of
football?" Ms. Hickens grabbed an orange
from the table. I laughed, "Football, I've
never played it. Do you have a ball?"

"We will make do with this orange."
She dropped the orange onto the floor and
kicked it over to me. "Don't let my
appearance fool you. I used to play sports
all the time in school," she boasted. I

gave the orange a little kick, laughing
about how silly this felt.

"Oh, you got to kick it harder than
that. With all your force; show me what
you got."

She kicked the ball back to me. I
threw my right leg back, swung it forward,
and kicked the ball as hard I could. The
ball flew high in the air, hit the
ceiling, flew back down, and rolled to Ms.
Hickens feet. She loved it.

"Think of your worst thought and kick
the orange back to me," she told me. I did
exactly that. I thought of the death of my
parents, being taking away from Claudia
and Tom, every slap and cigarette burn my
aunt gave me.

"Now don't you feel liberated?" She
kicked it back to me.

"Almost." I kicked it hard back to
her.

"How about now?" She kicked it to me.

I kicked it back to her. "Not yet. I
am letting all my angry out."

"I am in support of that. You kick it
all out." She kicked the orange back to
me.

My foot caught the orange with a hard
stomp. I got into a rhythm kicking the
ball back and forth to her.

"I almost feel it." My breath was
slipping away from me. But I kept kicking
the ball.

"Do not rush it out." She kicked the
ball.

"I'm not." I kicked back.

Ms. Hickens gave a kick that made the orange bounce to me. The worst feeling I had left me so upset. Tears almost developed in my eyes. The fact that I looked like my aunt and not my mother made me use all my might, kicking the orange so hard it flew into the air and went splattering in pieces of orange peel and juice that landed everywhere on me, Ms. Hickens and the furniture.

I yelled on top of my lungs, "I felt it. I got it all out. Yeesss." That was a good feeling. We were both jumping up and down screaming at the top of our lungs.

"That was a good kick. I think you have enough talent to play for a ball team."

"I could play, huh?" I was out of breath. We went down the hallway to find the orange we used for our ball. The orange spots on the wall led us to the beat-up orange in the corner of the floor. We laughed when we saw it. Ms. Hickens picked it up and tossed it into the trash. I grabbed a wash cloth out of the closet.

"Here you go." She handed me a bar of soap and turned on the sink faucet. "Wash your hands and your face real good." I did with a huge smile. My heart kept beating from the fun of kicking the orange to shreds. The orange juice that spotted the walls was the funniest thing I had ever seen.

The juice poured down to the floor,
making a man's shape looking like he had
legs of a spider. The little spider man
was running from something. His legs made
him run faster. I slumped down onto the
bathroom door in the middle of my wash up.
Scattered juice started to harden on my
face. I knew it wasn't the time for
devastating thoughts.

But the excitement had briefly
vanished from my heart and my grief took
over. The wrong person was on the other
side of the door waiting for me to
continue my fun with her; not my mother,
not my father, not Claudia and not Tom. A
stranger who took me in as I wandered into
her house allowed me to stay for a while.

"Well, we have to create more days
like this, being liberated as if nothing
is withholding us from feeling like a nice
cool breeze. How are you feeling now?"

"A little better," I let her know.

"Go finish washing yourself. So we
can start our liberating week."

She kissed my cheek, nodding to let
me know things were okay. Her hands were
soft like a baby's skin. Her eyes burst
with the kindness she was about to give to
me. I flew into her arms, hugging her
tightly. I felt lucky too.

"We are liberated women," she said in
my ear. The world didn't matter on the
outside.

The new imposer took over my body throwing the old one into the trash. The new one made my face brighten.

"Okay, I will be liberated with you."

"I hope you feel that way on the days you are not with me and all the time."

It was the week that liberated us. By the end of that week I did feel liberated, as if nothing could harm me or keep me in one place. Kicking that orange was a symbol of hope.

Watching it roll was a symbol of strength. Strength and hope represented in an orange was my sign. One day I would be on my own. I was strong enough to kick my way through anything.

Fears were only setbacks; I did not need anymore. After my wash, we relaxed in the living room.

"I wrote a lot of letters to my parents," I confessed to her.

"Was it better for you to write down everything?" She wanted to know.

"Yes, writing is my only communication with my parents. I think they get my messages faster if I write."

"I think so, too."

"Sometimes I read the letter out loud then throw it away."

"However you decide to talk with them is your own special way," Ms. Hickens said.

I knew my grandparents were Muslim. My parents opted not to belong to a religion. They were free thinkers who could not create their art under all the rules and obligations the religion had.

My father's father told him, he never heard of a Middle Eastern man not being Muslim. He could have at least disappointed and embarrassed him by becoming a Christian, but for him not to belong to any religion made my grandfather shake his head in shame. That's when my teenage father pulled out a permission slip for him to take a trip to Amsterdam. No words were spoken between them for a long time. I knew both of them missed each other, but they were too proud to say. My father left, too and did not come back. His father must have felt like Ms. Hickens.

"Writing sounds like a support blanket for you," Ms. Hickens said.

"What is a support blanket?" I asked.

"A support blanket is someone or something that supports you when you feel you have none," she answered.

"Oh so, we are each other's support blankets?"

"Yes we are."

"Okay, I have more questions."

"Bring them on; I'm ready to answer whatever question you have."

"Bring them on." There was a smile on my face. "What do you mean?"

She smiled back at me. "It is an expression for let me have all your questions."

We spent the rest of the evening asking and answering questions. I asked normal questions to the strangest. "This is for you. We will work this together."

Ms. Hickens brought out a map of the world, glue, scissors, and huge blank canvas.

"What will we be doing with this?" I asked, picking up the glue.

"We are going to fix a puzzle. Here." She gave me the scissors. "Cut off the countries so we can glue them together on the canvas. Then we can view what the world looked like when it was not separated by miles of oceans."

I cut as straight as I could along the lines. I wanted to get the perfect one world I could make. No one had ever told me of the things I was learning on my adventures with Ms. Hickens.

"I will try to do so, but you do not believe me."

My neighbor had always told my mother she could not wait to die because only then would she be able to rest. She wanted a rest from her loud month husband and hyper eight children he had begged her to have. I wished we were still neighbors. I would tell her that, according to our most influential thinkers, she would live forever or burn forever, and resting was not mentioned. She had better start resting as much as she could now. I would rather her rest in our garden than to suffer great disappointment. But we are not neighbors anymore and the thought made me laugh.

   Ms. Hickens stood. "Let us take a break and get a snack." The night had come and it looked like I was going to live with Ms. Hickens, laughing and learning forever.

Chapter 5

I laid in bed wondering why Ms. Hickens
looked at me the way she did when she
found out my birthday. I wondered with my
eyes wide open. I knew I didn't look my
age. My body had stopped developing
properly the day I moved in with my aunt.
I knew I looked like a little girl.

All afternoon, Ms. Hickens quizzed
me, ten out of ten better than my three
out of ten, I received back the other day.

"That's much better. Now we can
advance to the level you should be at. For
your age you should be a freshman in a
high school."

"Is that what America calls their
university schools?"

"Yes, A high school for students
between the ages of thirteen and
seventeen. Then you go to a university or
college for four years."

She thought I could go to college. I
looked at her curiously.

"I still have many books here that
would be prefect for you." She went to get
the books. "We will keep reviewing the
textbook you have in front of you and
these two, too."

Three textbooks were laid in front of
me. Ms. Hickens wanted to review the end
of the chapters and quiz me twenty

questions. She had a set time to finish, which normally ended in three hours. We would break between a lesson to eat or dance. There was no cable television for us to watch.

"You know what?"

"What?" I answered.

"I do not think it's healthy for a person to focus on one subject all day." She looked at me.

We were talking while making a fresh batch of muffins for the day. "We will split our time between subjects. In the morning we will focus on reading, afternoon math. In the evening we will explore our city New York." She allowed me to measure a cup of flour. I wore a chef's apron. Mixing all of the ingredients together made me feel as if I was a chef.

"Are you going to teach me about Science and English? We had a class for that at my old school." It had been five years since I had been to school. I knew my speech suffered and I was way behind the normal teenage girl. The years I had spent lacking nutrition had stopped my growth. I could have passed as a twelve-year-old girl, not a fifteen year old beginning her freshman year of high school in America. People could almost mistake me for a cancer patient before I met Ms. Hickens. Lucky no one ever saw me up close. Since I have lived with Ms. Hickens the color in my face started to appear again.

"You are right. You should know science and English. We are going to plan our stay around those subjects. We will spend an hour on each subject starting every morning at ten. You will be even more intelligent then you are now." I hoped she meant I would be even more intelligent times the five years I missed from being out of school. "Then you will be on your way into getting in college."

"Maybe I can go to college in a big city." My eyes widened as my hands expressed the word big.

"Sounds like a wonderful idea. What city would you like to go?"

"I do not know. Where is the best place for me to go to?"

"A lot of places focus on different things. You can go to an art school for art, a business school for business or a school for technology studies."

I listened to everything she said. All my choices seem to never end. Ms. Hickens told me there are schools for ballerinas to attend. I had always thought ballerinas were born with pointed feet. "I have a lot to choose from. I need the school that will make me a chief," I told her, pouring my liquid berry pastry into a muffin pan.

"You do not have to decide today. By the end of learning all we are going to learn, you will know which school is right for you."

We began our morning with reading. "Everything We Had," became our first book. The book was about a family who lost all of their possessions during the Holocaust. Ms. Hickens read first. "The next book you will read by yourself."

She gave me a list of spelling words to know by the end of the week. The next hour we will master math. I read a new chapter. Ms. Hickens reviewed it with me. Then I had to do independent studying. Before we ate lunch I had to help clean up the living room.

"Once you keep feeding yourself good healthy food, your body will develop," she told me.

I shrugged. My food sat there as I stared off to the wall. I knew I did not look like what a fifteen-year-old was supposed to look. I could not look at Ms. Hickens. I could not keep my head up.

"Oh, honey, I did not mean to get you upset. I am only trying to look after your health."

"I know it is hard to talk about."

"That is why we have to talk about it. So it won't be so hard. I say, if you don't say it out loud, then how will you hear yourself?"

"Hum." I began to eat. "I want to look my age. Do you really think I could still grow like a normal girl?" I put my fork down.

"Yes, your growth hasn't stopped yet." She answered me with a tone so smooth, it sounded like a song. I ate fork after fork without noticing. I wanted to feel normal and to look normal even more. After lunch Ms. Hickens read to me *An Introduction to Science*. The book showcased all the history of science everyone should know. My mother taught me English. She said it was just like learning French. My grandparents and father's native tongue was Arabic. Ms. Hickens quizzed me as I thought of my parents speaking to each other in their native parents' tongue. I felt more in a daydream of love that crossed between my parents' eyes. I saw my mother's smile making my father smile back at her.

"We can advance you to a higher level." She laughed a little.

"What is so funny?" I asked.

"When I taught at the high school, my students were all Americans, but if we were to give this simple quiz, only half of them would have been able to pass it. And they were born speaking English." She looked at me. "You are a stranger to our land and you speak it as if it was your own."

"My mother was a good teacher," I told her.

"That I believe." She agreed.

After finishing our English lesson, we embarked on a new travel, exploring another great place. Curiosity overshadowed my excitement to find out more about different places, as always.

Months passed and my life had surrounded itself with learning. Ms. Hickens thought watching television would ruin all the knowledge she installed in my brain. She only turned it on to watch an educational movie. The thought of my aunt's whereabouts lingered only for a second.

I hoped she was alright, as long as she did not come back for me. My empathy for my aunt was infrequent. I was alone only when Mrs. Hickens ran errands. It was at these times that I felt my aunt would appear and take me as her prisoner again and no one would know what happened to me. One day before Ms. Hickens could get to the door, I reached for her arm and held firm to it.

"I want to go with you. I have been ready to go out for a long time," I said affirmatively as I straightened my posture, "I am not a little girl. I can defend myself against the world." She slipped off her shoes and un-wrapped the scarf around her shoulders, gently removing my hand.

"Well, we will have to get you a dress. You can't go out looking like that." She smiled warmly at me and headed upstairs. Moments later, I heard water running. I stood in the doorway of the bathroom, watching her test the temperature of the water with her hand.

"May I pour your bubble bath soap into the tub?" I asked as I reached over the sink to get the tall pink bottle.

"Yes and you can put the bath pearls in the tub, too." She pointed to the bath pearls. The pearls popped into the water. A fresh lavender scent filled the bathroom.

"OH NO!" I screamed.

"Ok, what happ"

"I'll be right back," I interrupted as I rushed past Ms. Hickens and down the stairs.

"I forgot to take the muffins out of the oven!" I called behind me.

"Please do not scare me like that!"

I hurried to the kitchen. The smoke stopped me at the door.

"Oh no, no, no." My heart raced as I hoped the muffins were somewhat edible. Baking muffins in the morning became a daily routine. "Uhhmmm," I said with relief. My muffins had been saved. They were only a little burnt on the top. I just considered them to be well-cooked. I retrieved the tray I normally used to place my muffins on. Beside the muffins I placed a small dish of caramel sauce, a handful of berries, and a glass of green tea.

"Bellina, the tub is ready for you," Ms. Hickens yelled down the stairs.

"Here I come," I let her know. I grabbed my tray to head upstairs. As I reached the top, I could see Ms. Hickens

sitting patiently on the toilet awaiting
my return.

"I see you prepared a snack for your
bath," she said with a wink.

I smiled. "I thought it would be
better to go all the way." I set my tray
on the edge of the tub. "Take your time;
we will make it out today. I am going to
be in the living room. When you are
finished taking your bath, get dressed.
Make sure your clothes look nice"

"You want them to look nice? I still
have clean clothes to wear," I
interjected.

"I want them to be wrinkle-free."

"You mean you don't want them to have
any wrinkles in them?" I inquired. I took
off my clothes, then carefully climbed
into the tub. My eyes closed when the warm
water touched my skin. The heat of the
water felt like a massage on my body as I
slid down enjoying my bathwater.

"Yes, pick out your clothes and iron
them."

"Oohh kay," I agreed. Ms. Hickens
closed the door halfway.

"Do not forget to comb your hair!"

"I will not." I stayed in the tub for
a while. I dreamt of escaping to a beach
surrounded by white sands on a remote
island far, far away. Only a breeze would
wrap around me like a silk shawl.

French horns played a private concert
in the clouds. My feet sank into the sand,
leaving footprints as I danced to the

French horns. I twirled with my arms
flowing in the air. I was a graceful
ballerina on pointed toes dancing on the
white sands. I thanked the audience for
their applause after my performance. How
lucky I was to have fresh exotic fruit on
the one tree that stood on the island. I
ate after my performance. I invited a lone
starfish to the feast. We chatted about
the great weather the island had. He said
he lived on the island all his life. He
had never seen it so beautiful as today. I
am very lucky, I thought. The rest of the
day I lay under the fruit tree. The lone
starfish returned to his home.

My eyes wandered to the blue flowered
decorated ceiling. It was a mystery to me
why Ms. Hickens' son and wife would ever
want to disown her. She was so giving. She
had cared for me as if I were her
daughter. I could only imagine how much
more she would care for me if I were her
blood. I thought unless his wife's mother
was ten times more giving and caring then
Ms. Hickens, he did not make the right
choice. The chances of him marrying into a
family who treated a stranger like Ms.
Hickens treated me were slim to none.

Nothing seemed to be the right answer
to why they disowned her. Every now and
then Ms. Hickens talked about her son.
Those were the times she really missed
him. I stared at the ceiling waiting for
the flowers to move. There was no chance
of them changing colors either.

The purple flowers just stayed there gazing back at me. Little circles of rainbow colors appeared to be chasing each other. I blinked to disregard them. Ms. Hickens had taken me in because she was lonely. I was someone she could talk to. Soon, we would be able to converse like educated adults. She was a good teacher; I was an obedient student. I learned quickly. We had serious conversations about life, discussing the expectations I had for myself.

"Make no mistake; the world can be a mean place. I do not want you to ever allow someone to mistreat you," Ms. Hickens insisted.

"I won't!"

"Promise me no one will ever mistreat you," she reiterated with a commanding tone.

"I promise," I said as my eyes fill with tears. I could never go back to my aunt's house if Ms. Hickens expected me to keep my promise. I loved the worldly knowledge Ms. Hickens had provided. She reminded me of Claudia with her world explorations. Much like Claudia, she drank tea and ate small cakes all day long. My daydreaming images vanished quickly by a startled knock on the door.

"Bellina, are you about finished?" she said. I did not know how much time had passed. The water was still pleasingly warm.

"Almost … may I have fifteen more minutes?" I requested. My thoughts still lusted for more daydreaming. I had to preserve those images in my mind for a short time. This was my chance to let them out before preserving them again. Ms. Hickens, Claudia, and Aunt Michelle had enough stories to keep me dreaming all day. The story of the one who lost her son, the one who lost her best friend, and the one who beat an innocent child added such drama to my life.

All their stories swam above my head. They were flashes of colorful circles chasing each other.

All of them in one room would spark interesting debates that I longed to hear.

"I'm coming out now!" I called down to Ms. Hickens. The clothes I picked out to wear that day were more suited for my age. Ms. Hickens bought them at a department store for me. The sales woman told her every girl wore the style and insisted it would look fabulous on me. I had a white lace blouse, wide-leg blue jeans, and a black belt.

I had to iron my jeans and blouse. I took out the iron and plugged it into the jack. I didn't call on Ms. Hickens to help me. I wanted this achievement of preparing my clothes to be my own. The problem I had was I had never prepared my clothes on my own.

My mother always made sure my father and my clothes were clean, starched, and pressed. I never had a reason to prepare my clothing at my aunt's house. I laid my jeans on the bed. I stretched my jeans as taut as my arms could hold to decrease the wrinkles. I gripped the iron and smoothed it firmly over each pant leg.

I firmly pressed hard upon some stubborn wrinkles that had not changed with my movement. I pressed over them several times, but they remained a wrinkled mess. I removed the plug from the wall socket; it was broke. I continued stretching my jeans by hand. I then drifted to the living room. Ms. Hickens' speechless look said all it had to say to me. Before she started to speak, I began to feel a pain in the pit of my stomach. This was a familiar feeling. I took a breath and convinced myself there was nothing to fear. She wasn't my Aunt Michelle; she had already proven that.

"Hmm, I know I asked you to iron your clothes. What happened?"

"Uh … I did not use the iron; I stretched my clothes out by hand. I think the iron is broken."

"Are you sure it was the iron that didn't work? Maybe you did not know how to work it," she smoothly said.

"I do not know." I answered.

"Let's go back to the room and I will show you how to use the iron."

"Okay," I said as we headed back to the room. The iron sat in the corner where I had left it.

"First, we do not leave any hot metal on the floor," Ms. Hickens demonstrated to me how to correctly iron my clothes. She took her time, then turned it over to me, so I could show her what I learned. My jeans were crisp and smooth after she was finished. I laid them on the bed so we could admire them. She said to let them cool for a minute. After pulling them up to my waist, I caught a glimpse in the mirror. They looked really nice with my white-lace blouse. As we approached the door, Ms. Hickens wrapped a black shawl around my shoulders. The shawl was soft and warm.

"Now we are ready to go out into the city," she said as she opened the door. "You look beautiful, Bellina." My excitement burst through my heart. An explosion of feelings came in waves. Soon we would be caught in the rush of New York City.

"Stay close to me, hold my hand," Ms. Hickens insisted. She grabbed my hand as she pushed through the crowd of people on the street. My sightseeing consisted of dark button-up jackets and sweaters brushing past us swiftly. We walked fast to keep up with the pace other patrons seemed to be adhering to. My eyes widened as I almost walked into a man's crotch. I tripped on Ms. Hickens foot trying to squeeze myself behind her to avoid going face-first into a strange man's privates.

"Oh, be careful, Bellina." She told me.

"I am, I almost" I stopped myself, not knowing what to say. Explaining to someone in a crowd of loud people that I almost walked into a man's privates was not something you do in the middle of walking traffic.

"Okay, I will be more careful." I stayed nearly beneath her. I felt like a purse being tucked away in Ms. Hickens coat. I felt as if people's eyes were glaring at me, as if they knew a secret about me. I wondered what did they know, but for the most part, I kept looking down. I felt like I didn't belong in America and I wanted to belong. On every corner was a parked hot dog stand with small hand-friendly American flags.

"Can we buy an American flag?" I requested. She looked at me with approval.

"Sure we can," she permitted. We stopped at the next hot dog stand.

"Hello, I would like to buy a flag." The man behind the steaming metal box had a welcoming smile. His mustache was curled slightly as if he had been twisting it waiting for the next customer. His sallow skin and strong arms reminded me of my father.

"Here you go, little lady," he said gently as my cheeks flushed slightly.

"Uh … sir, how much will that be?" Ms. Hickens asked reaching into her purse to fetch her money.

"For you two … it's on the house." He smiled, winking his lazy eye at me. He looked like he enjoyed his work rather than the money he collected. At the end of the sidewalk, the light turned red for us to stop. I raised my hand, holding the flag in the air. I waved it left and right with such pride upon my face.

A couple of people smiled. Some clapped as I waved it with larger swoops. Ms. Hickens giggled when she realized what I was doing. For the people who could not tell I was a foreigner before, they could now. That did not keep me from waving and enjoying each wave I swung. Ms. Hickens pulled me into a door.

As we entered, the smell of fresh fruit and delicious food toured through the air. "I need to buy something for us to cook tonight." We had entered a mini-market that worked directly with farmers and fishermen. The mini market had free tasting for all the food sections it had. I approached all the vendors and went back a second time to a couple of them. Ms. Hickens stood debating; she always wanted the best brand at the best value.

"Bellina hold out your hands," she ordered and I obliged. I watched her pour the open box of oats into my hand. "Move your hand up and down." I did so slowly so I would not spill any on the floor. She examined the oats in my right hand closely. "I like the one on the left. What do you think?"

"Hmm, yes, I do too," I agreed. We chose the heavy white oats. I dumped them back into the box. We put the box into our cart.

"Corporate companies know how to use the system to get what they want. Everyone everywhere should be able to buy the best products at a reasonable price and not be forced to buy the products their class can afford. You see the box of the white oats had a much more appealing style than the other oats. Oh, why don't you go pick out something you'll like to snack on," she interrupted her own observation.

"Okay, what can I snack on?"

"Anything you like. Meet me at the checkout counter." She went to finish her shopping.

I twirled around to see what the mini-market had to offer me. Cookies, crackers, grapes, strawberries, candy-pops, cola, chips, apples, and oranges; I was only allowed to pick one. All types, all kinds of snacks were throughout the whole mini-market. They all lay in front of me, as I walked down the aisles. I took my time pacing up and down the aisle; I wanted to pick the perfect snack. One aisle was for cereal. I had never had cereal before. One box had oats with colorful marshmallows in it. One said honey nut crunch on it. I thought how nice it was to have so many different types of cereal. I wanted to snack on the cereal. I had made a choice. I remembered I had to get the best brand.

Otherwise, I would waste Ms. Hickens' money. She would lose it to the corporate companies. I opened the box of marshmallow oats and the box of honey nut oats. I poured a handful in my hand of the marshmallow oats, lifting my arm slowly as I did before with Ms. Hickens.

I examined its color and its weight. It looked good to eat right there. I poured it back into the box. I poured the honey nut oats into my hand. It looked okay. It wasn't as honey-colored as I had imagined it should be. The choice was clear to me. I put the handful of cereal back into its box as I did before.

"Excuse me, young lady, it's against the law to open any product in the store. You must pay for those two boxes you opened or the store manager will call the police!" The high-pitched voice startled me, and I dropped the open box of honey nut cereal on the floor. I saw at the end of the aisle a large man talking and pointing at me.

"Do you understand what I just said?" He nodded as he spoke. I looked at him like any other foreigner fresh off the boat. Without thinking, I rose on my tiptoes to reach his bending down face. I nodded as I answered him.

"I understood perfectly. Can you comprehend that the corporation that distributes these products should have products for everyone? Not just for the rich. If you call the police, I will tell them the same thing." I grabbed the flag that I had set down on the shelf during my examination and waved it slowly.

I waved it in his face, grabbed my brand-named oats with marshmallow cereal and ran. I threw the box of cereal in the cart Ms. Hickens was pushing. "I'll be waiting for you outside," I said quickly as I swiftly scampered away. I caught my breath outside. I looked to see if anyone was chasing me. I got away from the man in the mini-market.

"Aaahhhhhh!" I squealed. The rush that I felt racing through me made my heart thump hard in my chest. I hoped Ms. Hickens wouldn't be much longer inside the mini-market.

The city looked different as the sun reshaped its form. Model billboards, tall towers, and street jazz captivated the hearts of tourists. The city lights staged a show of architectural designs that played every night for the growing number of audiences. Each tourist I observed sprinted and pushed. They tried to find the perfect spot to view the horizon glistening over the mirrored windows of the skyscrapers.

"I got everything we need to make a fantastic dinner." She guarded the moonlight skies. "We should be heading back home before it gets to dark," she

informed me as she handed me the lightest
bag of groceries.

"Can we stay a little longer, please?
I am just now seeing how beautiful the
city can be," I pleaded with her.

"I, I am," I started again. "Let's
stay here for a moment, to see the lights
paint the city and finish their show," I
interrupted with my suggestion. I did not
want to leave. This was the first beauty I
found since I had been living in New York.
When the policeman took me through the
city to my aunt's house, the city had
looked so ugly and dirty. There was no
grace shown by anyone. The sidewalks were
painted with chewing gum; I couldn't walk
anywhere without watching where I stepped.
I wondered why people didn't throw their
gum into the trash cans that sat at every
other shopping door.

"Okay. We can take a seat over there
on that bench. We're only going to stay
out for a little longer, so we can make it
home in time to start dinner."

"Thank you," I said as I hurried to
the bench across from the mini market.
People shuffled past us as we sat; they
did not greet us. They all seemed to be in
a hurry. The night of lights had changed
the city from a duck to a swan. The image
of a beautiful white swan swimming on
clear crystal water appeared in my
imagination. It was so beautiful it made
me cry. This moment was magical. I knew my
father and mother had shared it with me. I

looked at Ms. Hickens, her eyes were filled with adoration as a tear stream down my face.

"I am ready to go now," I stated as I stood abruptly. I offered a hand to Ms. Hickens and gently pulled her hand so she could rise. We began our journey back home.

"I bought some books for you to read. I hope you like them." We carefully placed the groceries into the back of the car. We had a pleasantly silent ride home as we reflected on our special day. I pulled out one of the books when we were at home. Ms. Hickens began cooking her fantastic dinner for the two of us. The books were novels written for young adults. One was *The Girl Name Katie*. I took the book and sat at the table.

"Can we make time to go out every weekend?" I asked.

"Not every weekend. I do not think it would be good for you, and it will interrupt your studies. You've come so far, I can't allow you to get distracted." She moved a pot from the stove to the sink.

"Going out on the weekends can only help me more with my studies," I suggested.

Ms. Hickens was shaking her head.

"Why should I read about New York in my studies? We live in New York and can go see the places. I would experience the tastes, smells, and sights myself; not through someone else's descriptions. We can write our study of the city." I jumped out of my seat as my great idea burst from my brain.

Ms. Hickens stared at me proudly as she heard me voice my mind. It was as if she was viewing her works in developing a young woman reached its concluding chapters. My simple request had shown the difference from the girl who dreamed and the young lady who acts. We didn't need a book to explore New York; New York was in our backyard.

Chapter 6

Our weekend trips revealed the good and
the bad of the city. I got to see great
big buildings in the financial district.
The buildings didn't hold the financial
structure for only New York but held it
for the world, too. The large cities in
the world, rather than the countries, held
the most power. They controlled how wealth
was spent.

I caught sight of hundreds of girls
perched on corners waiting to be
discovered for the next Broadway hit. Some
were in line when my day began and were
still in line when my day ended. When
there were no more lines, I noticed a girl
run out of the double doors screaming, "I
got it! I got it!" Out of all the
hundreds, she was the one the city
discovered that day.

"One day that will be you," Ms.
Hickens told me.

"I am not a showgirl," I answered her
back. Girls who wanted to be in shows
wanted attention. I did not need
attention. But I knew if I ever wanted to
produce one of my plays, New York was
filled of attention-getters who would line
up before sunrise to get the part I was
offering. It was a good city to start at.
We walked past a shop that sold hats. On

the door was a sign that read HELP WANTED
APPLY WITHIN! Hhmmm, I wanted to work in a
hat store. I had to start paying for my
own meals somehow.

"Can I apply to work in the hat
store?" I inquired sincerely.

"You're too young to work, my dear,"
Mrs. Hickens told me.

"Why am I too young? I am able to
work like anyone else," I argued.

"By law, you are too young. You have
to be at least sixteen to be able to
work."

"May I still apply? I would like the
experience of learning how to apply for a
job," I charmed her. Reluctantly she
turned around and led me into the store.

"Hello, how may I help you today?"
the middle-aged woman welcomed us. Her
hair hid beneath a purple hat with a black
feather pointed out of the side. The dim
lights lit her glowing brown skin. Her
large brown eyes stood out. I could tell
she used a lot of lotion; it was the only
way her skin could glow that much.

"I would like to apply for the
position you have available." I walked
behind her to the counter.

"Great, I am so glad! Wait just a
minute." She glanced at me; her head fell
in a downward motion. "How old are you?"

"Hmm, I'm fifteen," I was truthful.
She giggled at me.

"You look a lot younger than fifteen,
and by law you must be sixteen to work."

She eyed me like a detective would eye a
suspect.

"Truly, I am fifteen; I just look
younger. I would like to apply for a job
to get the experience of applying," I
confessed confidently to her.

"Hmm," she said as she deeply sighed,
and handed me the application. "Fill this
out and come talk to me when you are
finished." She sounded enthusiastic about
my applying. She pointed for me to have a
seat at the table with the jar of pins.
"I'm Theresa, by the way. I own this
shop."

"Oh, this is your very own business?"
My voice grew to a high-pitched tone. I
looked at the black woman. This was all
hers. No one controlled her; she did the
controlling. I liked that. I brought my
focus back to the kind woman with the
purple hat as she handed me a pen.

"Yes, I've had this store for eleven
years," she said with a broad smile. Ms.
Hickens came to sit next to me.

"Are you from here?" Ms. Hickens
asked the store owner. She sat rubbing her
legs and twisting her feet around in
circles.

"I am … lived here my entire life,"
she told me.

I finished filling out the
application as they chatted. I wrote Ms.
Hickens as my guardian. The questions I
didn't know I left blank. The store's
phone started ringing. The randomness of

it startled me. I felt like I jumped out of my skin.

Theresa excused herself to answer the phone. I slid my application to Ms. Hickens.

"I do not know what these mean," I confessed as Ms. Hickens looked over my application.

"Okay … you filled out the first part right. You have the correct address. Hmmm, where do you go to school?"

"In your living room," I said with a snicker.

"So that means you are home-schooled. Yes, put that you are home schooled on that line."

"Okay and what about this one?" I pointed to the line for my social security number.

"Do you know your social security number?"

"What is a social security number? No one ever gave me that number."

"Hhmm, we will have to find out where you need to get yours."

"How come no one told me I needed one before?" My accent presented itself when I became apprehensive.

"Calm down, it'll be okay. Let's go to the next line. List your current and past employers; you should put N/A because you have never worked before."

"Okay, but if I got this job, worked here and went to apply for another job, then this job would go in the list for my next application."

"Yes, if you get this job and leave, you will be able to use this job on a list for employment for your next job," Ms. Hickens confirmed.

"Oh, thank you." I went to the next line.

"You are welcome, my dear."

"Should I get her to check my application?" I asked.

"Yes, you are doing this for an experience. Go to the counter, make sure you stand up straight and tall, like you are confident to start work today." I knew I wasn't there to start working. If I wanted to get experience, I had to do each step. Once I reached the counter, I handed Teresa the application.

"I filled it out as best as I could."

"Thank you," Teresa said as she glanced over the application. "I see you are being home-schooled."

"Yes, Ms. Hickens teaches me."

"Did you learn to speak all those languages from Ms. Hickens, too?"

"My parents taught me the languages."

"Aahh … I see," she said as she looked suspiciously at me, then at Ms. Hickens. "Where are your parents now?"

"They are in my heart and that is where they will always be." I never wanted them to leave my heart. I controlled the coming and going of their presence. The one thing I regret is not being in charge of their lives while they were still with me. I knew that sounded weird for me to control my parents' lives. They would still be alive and we would be happy if I was in control. It is a dream that snapped when my eyes widened. I was awake, standing at a counter, learning about applying for a job.

"Everything looks good, only always put your social security on your applications," Teresa said to me.

"I do not have an identification card," I confessed.

"That is a problem. You can't work anywhere without one," she advised me.

I thanked her for helping me with my experience and took my application with me.

"Good luck and come back when you turn sixteen and have your social security." She waved goodbye to me. Ms. Hickens was waiting for me by the door. There was nothing she could do about me getting an identification card. She was not my legal guardian under the law. I was sure my aunt threw all of my information away.

* * *

Ms. Hickens and I were sitting in the living room of her home. I did not feel quite comfortable. I wanted to run across the street to my aunt's house to find all the information I could and to get my identification card. I didn't exist without my information. I could end up depending on Ms. Hickens forever.

I looked at her. What if she died and I still did not have my information? Who would take care of me? I would end up by myself with nothing or no one. The stories we told, the places we traveled wouldn't matter if they were only in my head. I looked at the window; the wind had picked up and was whistling a high-pitch song. The house that was vacant for almost a year had the proof of my life in it.

A few leaves flew across the dark, gloomy house. I crept downstairs to peek out the window. I wanted to see if my aunt was at the front door about to enter the house she had abandoned. There was no need to wait for a light to come on; drunks hated the light. It forced them to see how pathetic they had become.

The moonlight made it possible to wait for her shadow to appear. Night after night I crept down the stairs to gaze out the window; no one came. Not even one of my aunt's neighbors came to wander around the house. Her booze and cigarettes, I suspected, were waiting for her by the door. Unfortunately, her life was like a piece of worthless trash easily thrown away. Being trash is worst then being dead. People remember and honor the dead. They dedicate their lives to protect and find justice for the dead.

The birthdays of the dead were still celebrated like they were still alive. People will eat cake as if their deceased loved ones are also devouring a piece next to them. Trash wasn't meant to be thought of, and for whatever reason my aunt had become that. After all the beatings she gave me and the cruel things she said to me, I was still awaiting her return, night after night.

"Bellina, have you been listening to me?" I jumped at Ms. Hickens' voice.

"I do not know, I heard you say a little but I did not hear the rest," I confessed.

"You have to pay attention or you will miss a lot of important things."

"I am sorry. I was just thinking we have to get my information from my aunt's house. So I will exist like everyone else!" There was no way I could concentrate on anything else but getting over to that house.

"Slow down, slow down." She put her hand on my lap to settle me. "What are you talking about?"

"I need my identification card to be able to exist. I know it is in my aunt's house."

"Oh sweetheart, you would not have an identification card. You may have a visa, I assume, with your other information, but you have to be a U.S. citizen to have an identification card," she stated while my face twisted with confusion. At this point, I just wanted something with my name on it. I felt my heart breaking by the minute.

"But I need to find my information to exist in the world!" I cried out.

"You do exist in the world," Ms. Hickens pulled me to her and held me tight, "I'm sure we will find all the information for you."

"Really, you believe so?" I asked for assurance.

"Yes, I know so. We will find your information this weekend."

"This weekend?" I yelled. "I must go now!"

"Oh, Bellina, it will be okay."

"No, it won't. Please we have to go tonight!" I pleaded.

"Alright, alright, we will go in the morning."

"The morning is so far away. I must go tonight!" I cried.

"The morning we will go. Now you must calm down," Ms. Hickens commanded.

Ms. Hickens wiped tears from my eyes. "There, calm down. You know sometimes we can't worry about the things we can't control." I had heard those words before from other people I loved. It didn't matter who said the words or the form in which they came; after they were said, I just worried more.

We stayed on the floor a little longer before Ms. Hickens got up to fix a cup of tea for us. I heard a voice whisper forcefully, Get to the house. Get to the house. Now! Go, go, and get to the house now, Bellina! The pot steamed as it alerted Ms. Hickens the water was hot enough to be poured into the green herd mix of flavored grass. I sat back trying to clear my head of the voices that moved into it.

"Hmm, timing is everything. Everything has its own way of working out all in due time. You can't rush it, darling," Ms. Hickens tried to convince me. Our cups were in front of us. I watched the liquid as it swirled in the cup. I mouthed in a whisper back to her.

"Timing is everything. Everything," I wanted her to say, Here, I found a way for you to get the documents you need. I wanted her to declare that due time was in thirty minutes later.

"Tomorrow morning we will find the information you need. If we don't it, on your eighteenth birthday, I will take you to the social worker assigned to your case. She should have all your information," she sincerely suggested.

"We can get my information from her!" I began to understand. Only my social

worker lived in Geneva. But I thought
maybe Ms. Hickens had connections.

"Yes, she will have to turn over your
information when you are eighteen. Now I
want you to finish your tea and stop
worrying."

"Even if my social worker stopped
coming to check on me, she would still
have my information?" I raised another
question to further my comprehension of
her proposal.

"Yes, that is her job, to keep a
record of you."

We finished our tea and went to bed.
I stayed awake throughout the night and
waited for the sun to rise and the day to
begin. At the very first glimmer over the
horizon I leapt out of bed, ran to the
bathroom to wash my face, threw on my
clothes as I pranced from room to room.

"Ms. Hickens, Ms. Hickens are you
ready?" I shouted as I banged on her door.

"Come on, I am ready!" she called out
from the door.

"I will be there in a minute. Are you
ready for your studies? You've never been
ready so early to start your studies. I'll
hurry up so we can begin our new lesson
today." I couldn't believe my ears; had
she forgotten our midnight conversation?

"Oh no, no, no, I thought we were
going to look for my information," I
desperately stated.

"We are after your lesson," she
indicated.

"Uhh it will be late in the afternoon then." I cried.

"It will be okay. Everything will still be there this afternoon. But our responsibilities must come first. And your responsibility is to learn," she said firmly.

I opened my mouth to protest, but ran to the living room instead. I shouted back to her. "Ok I am starting my studies. Please hurry to assist me!" I flipped open to the page that

Ms. Hickens had marked with a Post-it. I pretended to read, only caring about getting to the house that hid my information. Minutes turned into an hour as my wait went well into the morning. Finally, Ms. Hickens' door opened.

"Uhh I thought you would never come out. Why would you wait so long knowing how important this is to me?" I wanted to make her feel guilty.

"I am sorry, honey. I felt so awful this morning. My back was in so much pain." Ms. Hickens said.

"Oh, I'm sorry you're in pain. Are you better now?" I asked.

"I feel a little better. Thank you for asking. What have you been reading?" She sat next to me rubbing her back.

"I have not read anything," I told her truthfully.

"I see. You really want to go back to that house," She asked me with a worried look in her eye.

I sprung up off the floor, "Oh really, we must go!" Before she could say anything, I had sailed out the door. I heard her yell, "Hold a minute, let me put my shoes on!" But I was gone.

I ran across the street and stood at the front of my aunt's house. I felt a chill run up my spine. Dirt and cobwebs had formed on the house and on the door. The dirt had darkened the door color. The agony I felt standing there, scared to go in of what I might find, overwhelmed me. My stomach turned upside-down, making me want to vomit everywhere. I covered my mouth. I controlled my eyes from rolling back into my head.

"Ouhhhhh," I moaned as I inhaled several deep breaths, turning away from the house. The nearest tree was in the next yard. I ran to it, hoping no one would see me take their leaves.

I pulled some leaves from the tree. I wasn't going to open the doorknob with my hands. I wiped the cobwebs off and twisted the door knob with leaves as a protective glove. The door squeaked open. From the smell of the house, I knew the house had been empty since I had left it almost a year ago. The unpleasant scent knocked me back a couple of steps. It made my stomach turn and twist worse than before. I sat in front of the house to get the few deep breaths I had left.

"Aahhhh!" I screamed at the top of my lungs, jumping up and shaking my hands. A rat scampered across my shoe in an effort to escape the prison I knew so well. The house wasn't inviting as the door stayed open. I was taking back to what my life was like there.

I heard the silent sympathy playing on a broken record repeatedly. I envisioned the empty bottles of what used to be vodka being aimed at the wall hitting me. Heavy pounds of her balled fists marked me still. I wasn't there for more heartbreak; I was on a mission to secure my proof of existence.

With that determination, I entered the house. Dust painted the house from wall to wall. The odor of that was left behind forced my shirt to act as a mask. Yes, the house was left abandoned by my aunt and me. My eyes shut to keep all of the dust from irritating them. I fought my way to the bathroom.

I turned on the faucet. No water came out. The bills hadn't been paid. There were no letters of eviction notices on the door. It was just part of being trash, I thought. Not even the realtors came to get their house back. The more I thought, the more I realized I didn't have time to wonder.

I ran upstairs into the room I had entered one time before. If there was anything, about anything it would be protected in that room. I looked in the drawers. To my surprise, neatly folded blouses lay in the first two drawers, blouses of colors and prints; beautiful blouses for a young lady. Women's lingerie lay neatly in the third drawer. The other two drawers were empty. Jeans and skirts hung in the closet.

There were no signs of any papers containing my information. I looked under the bed, in her shoe boxes, and on top of her closet. I found nothing. I was sweaty and hot from not having any light or fresh air. All the dust in my eyes only made me start to cry. I couldn't say if it really was the dust making me cry. I fell on the floor trying to hold back the tears. I heard heavy breathing. I felt my heartbeat deepen as I jumped when then a shadow too thin to be Ms. Hickens appeared over me.

Chapter 7

"I have found nothing," I revealed my result with a disappointed look out the window. The road looked like it continued forever.

"Why don't we come back this weekend and look through the whole house? That way we can search with four eyes instead of only two."

"Four is definitely better than two. The house is dusty and dirty. I could barely see in here." I turned to face her. She wiped some dust from my cheek, escorting me out of the house.

"That is why you didn't find anything because you didn't clean the house."

"Clean the house?" I sounded like I had never heard of cleaning a house before. My eyebrows rose.

"Honey, you are never going to find anything important in a dirty house. You have to field clean the house. Saturday … Saturday we will field day the house from top to bottom. Then we will search for your information."

"Ms. Hickens," I said with sincerity as I touched her hand upon her lap.

"Yes, baby?" she responded.

"What is a field day?" I asked.

"A field day is like spring cleaning, only it gets to the root of cleaning. Now does that sound like a plan for us to do on Saturday?" She slightly hugged me.

"Yes, it does." I smiled. I was on my way to victory. She took me from night to day all in an instance. I was back in comfort, away from the pain my aunt caused me.

"Go clean yourself, then you can eat the dinner I cooked for you."

"Oh, nooo!" I jumped up and raced to the bathroom. I was starving with hunger pangs to prove it.

"I'm glad you are excited because you still have to make up for today." She called after me.

"Uhhggg!" I said in frustration.

"I know how you feel. Now, I want you to read chapter fourteen before you go to bed," she said.

"From which book?" I asked.

"From all of your books, you should be on or close to chapter fourteen in all of your studies." I glanced over to the stack of books. "You do not have to read it all tonight." I looked at her with my eyes wide open with surprise. "Scratch that idea. I want you to write an essay."

"On what topic?" I asked

"What do you plan on achieving in the next five years?" she disclosed. I repeated what she said.

"What do I plan to achieve in the next five years?" With my thoughts swimming rapidly, I had no idea. Five years was enough time for something to happen or maybe nothing at all to happen.

"Why five years?" I requested her reasoning.

"You should have a goal of where do you want to go, what you will you be doing, and how much savings do you want to have. I want you to have goals and be successful in your life. Five years is enough time for you to achieve it," she explained while we fixed ourselves plates of food.

"What if I wanted to stay here with you?" I said.

"I will have the police escort you out," she stated sternly, then smiled. I didn't think it was funny. "You are welcome to visit, but I do not want you living on this block. Your mind is too full to keep living here." She put her fork of food in her mouth. "Don't rush through, but think carefully. I want you to type the essay," she instructed.

I wasn't eating. Really I didn't want to stay here. I wanted to travel and see the world. "When should I have the essay completed by?"

"Friday at ten a.m." It was clear I had a couple of days. "Approximately 500 words on what you want to achieve and how you are going to achieve it."

"Okay," I agreed. I started slowly eating. Ms. Hickens went to bed. I volunteered to wash the dishes. The next five years of life was a mind-blowing concept. I saw myself finishing school, becoming a chief of a five star restaurant, and traveling the world. My dreams never stopped.

Finding out more about my abilities and interests was what I wanted to achieve in five years. I needed a day to think of my options. I had a plan; that was a start. I had to find out the college I wanted to go to and how I was going to get there. I wanted to go to the best college for culinary. Throughout the night, I stayed up outlining my thoughts.

"Good morning. I see you had a productive night," Ms. Hickens woke me. I was sleeping on the living room floor. "You are going to have to learn to manage your time. Staying up all night isn't good for you."

"Mmmmhh," I moaned as I crept up to a sitting position. A stack of papers fell off me. I slowly put them back together in the order I thought they were before I fell asleep.

"While you were sleeping, I started making breakfast. Hurry upstairs to wash up. By the time you come down, breakfast should be ready, then we will start our lesson."

"Okay," I said as I yawned dragging myself to the bathroom. I fell asleep on the toilet for an hour before I actually woke up to wash myself and get dressed.

"Hmm, are you sure you washed up?"

"Yes."

"You have been in the bathroom long
enough. You look so tired. Your food is
cold now. Go warm it up and eat quickly so
we can get started on today's lessons." I
stared at the plate a long time before
deciding I wasn't hungry.

"Well, if you are not going to eat,
let's not waste time."

"I'm ready to work." I started to go
over to the couch. "Give me one minute," I
requested as I hurried to the kitchen. I
gulped a glass of orange juice.

"Hmmm." I sighed at the refreshing
quench of satisfaction the juice gave me.
I gulped two more glasses down. I snatched
a muffin before leaving the kitchen.

"Huh, you look ten muffins better,"
Ms. Hickens teased me. I had a mouthful.

"Nothing is wrong. I just need to go
outside for some fresh air."

"May I come with you?"

"Yes, I think that's a good idea. We
both need to take a break and get out of
the house for a moment." I was joyous
about going out. Exchanging my studies for
fresh air was an exhilarating thought. The
door opened and I ran outside.

I paid no mind to the house across
the street. The mysterious papers that
were disintegrating gradually inside the
empty house didn't enter my mind. Like I
expected, the air felt clean; it smelled
like I was trapped in a rain forest with
nothing but wild tall trees swinging the
breeze my way. My nose twinkled when the

air brushed against my cheeks. I didn't care.

I was having the time of my life outside. I wasn't doing anything but enjoying the weather. I glanced around. Ms. Hickens sat on her porch, and I went to sit next to her. We swayed in her porch swing. My legs dangled freely as I rhythmically pushed off with my feet. Lucky for us the day was clear.

"I want to be a great chef," I declared to her.

"Why is that?" She looked down the road. There were a few people walking down the street.

"I want to make great cuisine that looks beautiful and tastes delicious. I just have to figure out where to go to school."

"We can find out what school you should go to together." She placed her hand on mine.

I had to review my statistics out loud. I had to do a public speech on how we could use statistics in our everyday lives. Then I had to use different formats for an example of everyday use. Each subject I was learning was paired in a group: math and science, art and music, literature and English, language and travel. That was my whole day with lunch in between.

Since my language skills needed little refreshing, we spent little time on

them. Our next travel was to Brussels. I
selected the city.

"I heard, in Brussels, we can eat
escargots on the streets. It's kind of
like how people eat hot dogs on the
streets here." I was so excited; Claudia
had talked about Brussels like it was her
world. It was so beautiful and innovative.
I laughed giddily. "We will have to eat
them. I love escargots!" Ms. Hickens
looked worried; she had never tried them.

"I would try them in a restaurant,
but I do not know how they would taste off
a street vendor," she said skeptical.

"Well, Claudia said they are sooo
delicious. She was my mother's best
friend. If she says they are delicious,
they are," I told her.

"Hmmm … I don't know."

"Hmmm, you eat a hot dog on the
street; why not expand yourself to high-
class food you can buy off the street?"

"Okay, I will try it only once," she
said.

"And fall in love." I wanted her to
fall in love with them.

"Now I didn't say that. I said try.
Let's not get our hopes up," she said
laughing.

"Don't worry. This is all about the
adventure of traveling right?" I dragged
my words, knowing she would agree with me.
She did not comment. "After all, there are
far worse foods in far worse places we

could be eating. Lucky us, we get to taste street escargots in Brussels."

"I think you should become a chef in a four-star restaurant," she suggested. I stared at the picture of escargots. Maybe I will, I thought.

We started to set up a cute little European town that represented Brussels in Ms. Hickens' living room. Our town was decorated quite nicely. It was a long step away from our first travel to Casablanca.

"Oh shoot, I forgot to pay the water bill today," Ms. Hickens remembered. "I guess I'll have to do that first thing in the morning."

"So, tomorrow we will have a late departure to Brussels from New York," I stated our schedule.

"That is the plan," Ms. Hickens said. "Since we won't be leaving until late tomorrow, how about we watch a movie tonight?"

"I would like that. Do we have popcorn?"

"You may have some popcorn," Ms. Hickens said. I jumped to get it. As it popped, I yelled to Ms. Hickens from the kitchen, "I think I should start cooking, to get prepared for culinary school."

"You can start tomorrow," she answered back. I brought the large bowl full of popcorn to the living room, putting it in the middle of us.

"Thank you," Ms. Hickens said.
"You're welcome."

The movie we watched was interesting; it was a two-hour movie. I crunched on the popcorn the whole time.

"That was a good movie," Ms. Hickens said yawning. She glanced in my direction. I knew she wanted me to go to bed.

"I can fall asleep," I informed her.

"Me, too. That's why we should call it a night and head to bed. We have to pay the water bill first thing in the morning."

"Then it's off to Brussels," I reminded her.

"Good night," she said.

"Night," I told her on my way to bed.

We started our trip to Brussels doing what we usually do. We read through our books, prepared a fitting meal, and celebrated the culture. We tried to speak in French throughout our entire journey. Ms. Hickens kept her French in an hour book most of the time. The basic things, she knew. I didn't need the book. I spoke it like I was speaking with my mother. Our first stop was at the Flower Market.

I loved all the beautiful flowers. The lilies were my favorite. I drew images of lilies and sunflowers to hang in the house. The house smelled of floral essence. We walked past the Grand Place taking pictures. After a day of walking through the city, we found our street escargots. Before we paid the bill, Ms. Hickens and I went to the store and she

got me fresh escargots. I soaked them in
butter and sautéd them before we ate them.

"Okay, now you have to try these.
They smell so good." I took one off the
plate and popped it into my mouth, rolling
my eyes backward, indicating how good the
taste was.

Ms. Hickens slowly picked one up and
put in her mouth.

"Uh-huh, it is okay. I wouldn't eat
it every day," she said.

I smiled, continuing to eat more.
They were so salty with a burst of butter
when I bit down. Heaven became real to me
that day. The meal had to be a Belgian
family meal.

"Belgian waffles, I will make next,"
I suggested.

"Sounds perfect to me," she said
sighing. We ate Belgian waffles and eggs
for dinner.

I had to present my essay to Ms.
Hickens about my goals for the next five
years. I wrote a good essay in my eyes. I
knew Ms. Hickens would like it.

"Read it out loud, please," she
requested as she passed my paper back to
me. I stood in front of her, ready to make
my presentation.

"The things I want to achieve within
the next five years consist of me starting
my life independently in a profession that
I love. When I came to America…" I read
the entire essay out loud. I added bits of
my life before I moved here. I told Ms.

Hickens that her cooking inspired me to become a chef because her food smelled so good. Once I was finished, I stood waiting for her to say something. She stood and started clapping.

"Bravo, you spoke very well," she said with pride brimming in her eyes. I felt good. All my words came from my heart. My words captured an audience, I imagined. Ms. Hickens had tears in her eyes. She gently wiped her face with a kitchen towel she had been holding.

Saturday finally came; the morning took forever to begun. I ate in a hurry and gathered our cleaning supplies while Ms. Hickens finished getting ready. We went across the street to field day the house. This is my duty I needed to accomplish this weekend. I was on a mission to do it. We started with the downstairs and worked our way up. We washed everything. We dusted everything.

"You know, I was thinking, a good way for you to earn money is to sell the make-up brand, Daze. You can work from home," Ms. Hickens shared with me. "I used to do it when I was pregnant with my son. I made pretty good money doing it."

"How do I get started?" I asked.

"I will set you up with a representative whom I have known for years. She will get you started."

"What if she says I'm too young?"

"Then you will work under me. How does that sound?" she asked in a cheery tone.

"Like a plan."

"Good!" The idea solved the working situation for the moment. I let Ms. Hickens do all the worrying about it. I would rather sell under her. I focused on cleaning the house. I scrubbed harder and faster than I ever could have imagined. When we were finished cleaning the inside, we had time to clean the outside before we lost all of the sun's natural light. We went home exhausted from the work and hungry from not eating all day.

"You must eat. It's not healthy to go to bed on an empty stomach," Ms. Hickens insisted. I was so tired; I found it hard to lift my fork to my mouth. I ate and went straight to bed.

The next day I woke early and left Ms. Hickens a note to meet me at the house. By the time she arrived I had searched all of downstairs. I had searched through the papers and books we pulled out.

"I am so sorry. I didn't realize how late it was." Ms. Hickens asked for forgiveness.

"It's okay. I haven't found anything yet," I told her.

"I will start looking in the other room." She headed into the room across from the one I was in. I thought of my aunt being much happier with a smaller house. It was freaky how the other room was decorated for a young boy. My aunt didn't have any children, let alone did it seem like she wanted any. Ms. Hickens and I searched and searched throughout the whole house. We were leaving when I stopped in the hall.

"Wait right here!" I ran back into my aunt's room. There was one box I didn't think of until a split second before our departure. There was a wooden box with a lock on it next to my aunt's bed. We didn't even see it. It stayed there untouched.

Ms. Hickens was speaking to me from the door. I didn't hear her. I was focused on opening the box. I shook it and tried to pull it open. Nothing worked. I was so frustrated that I picked it up and threw it hard across the room, causing it to break open.

"Bellina," Ms. Hickens reprimanded with her tone.

"Huh, huh, mmhhh," I muttered as I caught my breath. To my astonishment, pictures and letters laid between the broken wood.

"Oh, my God," Ms. Hickens said as she gasped in disbelief. She was speechless, as was I. I picked up a couple of the letters.

"My dearest Michelle… If times are tough let me help… I love you, we all do…

We will get through this one day at a time. Just let me help."

I read aloud as puzzlement came over my face. I picked up more letters until I found one I had never wanted to see.

"Nnooooo," I cried. The pain that stabbed my heart was worse than any beating I had suffered. "They all lied to me. Those lying, lying, liars," I screamed as tears streamed down my face. "No, no, no, nnnooooo!"

Ms. Hickens tried to calm me. But no one could. I did not have it in me to let them. My rage could handle any army that stood in my way. I snatched all the pictures and letters and took them with me. My eyes ached in pain as I tried to choke up my tears.

"We should go." She put both her hands on my shoulders as I sat in disbelief staring at all the letters and papers scattered on the floor. The documents rewrote my history, my life as I knew it. I wished I had never come back to the house. Ms. Hickens helped me to my feet.

"This can't be true," I insisted.

"Why don't we go home and make some hot chocolate and we can figure this out later tonight." She led me to the door. I stood in the doorway as she went to pick up all the papers off the floor and the rest that were in the drawers. We left with the stack in Ms. Hickens arms. I

didn't look back when we closed the front
the door.

   "I'll put these up. We can look
through them when you are ready."

   I sat on the couch. My face had a
burning tingly sensation. All the pressure
exploded throughout my face. I was angry
at the world, for all the lies I found
out.

   "Bellina, take a bath. I'll bring you
a cup of hot chocolate."

   I went to the bathroom without a
word. I sat on the toilet as the water
poured into the tub, thinking of my whole
life. The night went fast into the
morning. I woke with the sun shining on my
face. It wasn't a bad dream; the nightmare
had stayed with me. One day I would face
my aunt and all I found.

   "Belllina." Ms. Hickens knocked on my
door.

   "Yes?" I answered her.

   "May I come in?"

   "Yes, you may." I sat up in the bed.
Ms. Hickens had a glass of orange juice in
her hand and a stack of papers in the
other. She sat at the edge of the bed,
handing me the orange juice.

   "I thought these papers may come in
handy."

   I gasped at the papers she gave me.
Me! They were documents of my birth, my
visa, my existence. I didn't notice the
papers during my search. I was glad Ms.
Hickens did. Now all of my questions were

answered, except for one; the one that rewrote my history, the one I may never get an answer to.

"These are all of my papers!" I said

"All of your information is right here." Ms. Hickens looked at the papers. "I thought you might want these, too." She reached behind, bringing the letters from behind her back. A rush of anger flew over me. I was angry about the secret in the letter. The secret made me rethink my life and all who surrounded it.

"Did you read any?" I reached to take the letters.

"I didn't read the letters, only your documents."

I handed the letters back to her. "It is okay. You can read them." I was told before that time healed all wounds. The saying must have meant physical because I just did not know how time was to heal an emotional wound.

I did know how a person could time an emotional wound to heal. It was why I allowed Ms. Hickens to read the letters, because no matter tomorrow, or the next year or a decade later, I will still hurt by the news. Ms. Hickens put down one of the letters.

"Your aunt is a very hurt woman. She has a lot of pain in these letters, but that doesn't excuse the pain and abuse she put you through." Ms. Hickens held my hand and placed her other hand on my cheek. "No one deserves to have anyone hit them or verbal or emotionally abuse them. Though she has hurt you and you may never forget the things that happened, you should never stop living your life and going after the things you want because of what she did to you."

"What about the secret?" Tears rolled down my cheeks into Ms. Hickens' hand.

"Oh, honey, don't allow that to stand in your way. Of course family secrets can hurt, but what did I tell you?" She nodded as she opened her mouth to say, "Do not allow it to stand in your way. Say it with me."

"Do not allow it to stand in your way."

"Do not allow it to stand in your way" we softly chanted.

"Now say it by yourself. I won't allow it to stand in my way," Ms. Hickens said.

I cleared my throat. "I won't allow it to stand in my way." I said it until my tears dried up and my insides felt the load of my sadness had been lifted.

"You look like you feel a little better."

"I kind of do," I said with a smile.

"Why don't we relax the rest of the day?"

"That would be good."

"We can read," She suggested.

"How about we cook?" I interrupted excitedly. "It would help me take my mind off of things and prepare me for culinary school."

Ms. Hickens laughed, "Sounds great to me. What should we cook?"

"You have lamb in the freezer." I tried not to smile big. I really wanted to eat the lamb. I hadn't had it in years.

"How would you cook it?"

"Hmm, I don't know," I answered.

"Let's find out."

I assured myself I wanted to be a chef; like Ms. Hickens said, 'nothing should stand in my way.' I made it my goal to become a chef, "How about we roast the lamb?" I knew nothing about roasting. I was willing to learn.

"Sounds good. I have some season vegetables to go with the lamb." Ms. Hickens brought out the vegetables, the spices, and the lamb. I got the pots, pans, and utensils needed. We were ready to begin. I watched her measure and pour. I got to mix and stir the spices, then coat the lamb with it.

"How do you feel about cooking? Does this still make you want to become a chef?" she asked me.

"I still like it. I will tell you after we finish creating this meal." Truth be told, I didn't need to think about it; becoming a chef was what I wanted. The lamb smelled of rosemary, and curry spices filled the room. We used a small pinch of honey to rub on the lamb. I could smell the honey in the air as well. All of the spices reminded me of autumn. I loved autumn; the season made me feel good, like the way the food made me feel.

"How's the lamb coming along?"

"Great! Can you smell it? It smells so good!"

She laughed, "Yes, it does. You did a great job."

"Thank you. Dinner should be ready in fifteen minutes. I'll set the table." It was as if we were going to have a feast for the first time, forgetting about any trouble we ever had. A new beginning with hopes of a better happily ever after, I thought.

"Ready!" I called to Ms. Hickens. We sat down, eyeing the steam from the lamb. The vegetables had beautiful colors that brought life to the table. Ms. Hickens made mashed potatoes. She allowed me to make the dessert. We ate the feast with smiles.

"How do you like it?" she asked me.

"It tastes great!" and it did.

After dinner, we cleaned the kitchen, then fell onto the couch. We were stuffed like big old ladies. "I cannot move," I confessed. When Ms. Hickens laughed, I knew she couldn't move either. I laughed with her, thinking we were big old ladies. The rest of the day we stayed on the couch.

Time had made things go back to normal. Ms. Hickens taught me everything she knew. I wrote, I read; we ventured out

to many places around the city. I was
lucky to have Ms. Hickens in my life. I
didn't know where I would be without her.

I started working for Daze under Ms.
Hickens. We bought a kit filled with
makeup. I trailed along with Ms. Hickens
as we went to host parties trying to sell
the Daze products. At the end of every
party, I ended up leaving with makeup on
my face, marketing the products we were
selling.

Ms. Hickens put the money we
collected from Daze aside for me. I had
money, and my savings was growing. I paid
to take an upcoming test for college
entry. I couldn't wait because the test
would put me one step closer to achieving
my dream of going to culinary school. When
I wasn't working doing the Daze, I was
preparing for my exam.

I needed my identification card in
order to take it. I felt glad that I did.
The high school was not far from Ms.
Hickens home; I could walk there, but Ms.
Hickens didn't want me to. I arranged to
take my exam over the phone. I couldn't
wait for it because then I would be able
to apply to a culinary school. I didn't go
to bed easy, waiting for the morning of my
test date.

* * *

Hummingbirds woke me in the morning, singing and flying around my window. The sun beamed rays of shine throughout every corner in my room. I slugged out of the bed. My excitement had left and fatigue took over.

"Good morning, are you ready for your test?" Ms. Hickens bounced around the living room cheerfully.

"No, I could sleep a little longer, though." I sat at the dining table.

"Nonsense, you will do well. I have faith in you. Eat, then let's get ready to go."

I ate slowly, more playing with my food. On the way to the school, I rolled down my window, sticking my head slightly out, inhaling the breeze the wind pushed by. I closed my eyes, telling myself I can do this.

"We are here. Would you like me to go in with you?"

"No, I'll be fine. Will you wait for me?"

"I'll be right here."

The test took place in a plain white wall classroom. Other kids joked around as I waited for the test to begin.

A blonde-haired, tall woman came into the room, with test booklets in her hand. "Okay, everyone, and calm down. I'll pass out your test. You may begin once everyone has one. There's no talking, eating, drinking, or getting up to move. Please have two number two pencils out."

By the time she placed my test booklet in front of me, I was ready to begin. I had this burst of power within that I could pass this exam.

"Bring your exam up when you have completed it. Now you may start." She took a set behind the desk. I opened the booklet and started to fill in my name. Before I knew it, I had finished the whole booklet. I'm done! The thought of being done, raced through my head. I looked up and I was the only one sitting.

"Are you finished?" the woman asked me.

"Yes." I got up to take her the exam. "How long does it take to get the results?"

"Within the next two days. It will be mailed to you." She smiled slightly.

Ms. Hickens stood outside the car, opening the door for me. "How do you feel you did?"

"I think I passed." I hugged her with a huge smile. The next two days I waited on the couch for the mail to come. Once I saw the mail driver, I rushed out. "I'll take the mail!" I called to the mailman. Each day, no mail came for me.

"Bellina, it will be here soon. The mail isn't going anywhere," Ms. Hickens assured me.

"I know, but I can't eat or sleep until I know I passed." A knock on the door made me jump. I ran to open it.

"Ask who it is." It was too late; I opened the door.

"Hello?" A middle-aged man in a brown uniform stood at the door. "I have a certified letter for a Bellina Asma."

"I'm Bellina Asma!"

"Here you go, just sign here."

Ms. Hickens stood behind me. "Thank you," we said. I eagerly opened the envelope that was sealed shut.

"It's my results," I yelled.

"Did you pass?"

"We are pleased to inform you, Bellina Asma, have passed your college entry exam." I couldn't finish reading the letter; I was jumping with joy.

"Oh, congratulations! Let's celebrate! I'll cut us a slice of cake." Ms. Hickens went to the kitchen. I dropped the letter, jumping up and down from the excitement. I held on to the door to pick it up, pulling myself up.

I froze as the smile on my face had vanished. My lips felt like they were forced open and wouldn't close. I froze as we stood staring at one another. She looked like a frail ghost, barely able to cover her body with the torn dress she wore. She took a step forward and I gripped the doorknob tighter.

My heart pounded in my chest; I was frightened she was coming for me. I wanted to run, but my feet didn't move. I saw the fury in my aunt's face as she took another step. I knew she was coming for me.

Chapter 8

"Ahhhh," I screamed at the touch laid on
my shoulders. My chest exploded like a
boiling fireball, "I-I saw her," I said
chokingly.

"Who, baby, did you see?" Ms. Hickens
said, worrisome.

"Aunt Michelle, she was standing
right there. She walked toward me." I
pointed to my aunt's closed front door.
"She's coming to get me."

"No, honey, she isn't there and I
will never allow her to take you. You had
just a short vision." Ms. Hickens pulled
me inside, closing the door behind us.

"It was real. I saw her for real," I
told her.

"Sometimes fear will bring dreams or
visions, especially if something good is
happening in our life. It is not real,
just your vision is just a short setback.
You can overcome it."

"How do I do that?" I asked her,
breathing at a calmer rate.

"By continuing to go after what you
want by, living your life. Have you
decided where you would like to attend
college?"

I was glad she changed the subject. I
sat back on the couch, soaking between the
cushions. "There's this French culinary

institute in Paris, but it costs too much. So, I thought about going to the community college here and taking their culinary program."

"Nonsense," she roared excitedly. I looked at her, confused. "Don't you want me to go to college?"

"I do, of course. I want you to go to the college of your choice," she said.

"How should I pay for it?"

"When my son left, he never looked back. It hurt me so much when he left. The money I was saving for him, I still have. I want you to have it." She smiled at me. I was shocked. "You really want to give it to me?"

"To pay for your education, yes; I'm proud of you, and you deserve to have a chance to become a great chef."

I flew into her arms, hugging so tightly, "Thank you," I told her with tears in my eyes. I heard Paris calling my name miles away. All my documentation was in order, and I existed in the world. Best of all, Ms. Hickens paid my school and gave me extra money for rent and food. I also had some extra money from working for Daze.

"Surprise," Ms. Hickens shouted at the top of her lungs. "I wanted to do something special for you since this will be our last time together for a long time." She made dinner. A three piece layer caramel cake sat in the center of the table. Presents were wrapped for me to open. She took pictures as I opened them. To kick off my culinary career, I had received a leather encasement of chef's knives and a top of the line collection of sauce pots.

"Ohh, thank you. When did you find the time to hide everything? These are beautiful," I was amazed.

"While you were sleeping," she confessed, tasting the cake.

"I am not a deep sleeper!"

"I know, so I put sleeping pills in your juice to make sure you went to sleep."

"Uhh?" My concern rose slightly. "You have been drugging me?"

"Only in good faith, my dear. Now, let's eat and celebrate your first achievement."

We celebrated my achievements all the way to the airport. We sang songs and reminisced about our time together.

"Flight 283 to Paris, France is now boarding at gate eleven," a loud voice echoed through the terminal. The announcement made me and Ms. Hickens hold each other tighter with tears in our eyes.

"I love you so much. I am so proud of you." She kissed both of my cheeks, crying as she gave me one last squeeze. "You have to go so you can achieve the rest of your goals, and I will see you again when it is time."

"Okay, I love you so much, too."

"Let me look at you. You are a woman, a beautiful woman." My hand held her heart as she took control of herself.

"Now boarding Flight 283 to Paris, France at gate eleven," the voice echoed again with urgency.

"Thank you, I love you, I love you. I love you."

"Call me no matter what time it is," she requested. I waved back to her at the gate.

Flight 283 to Paris, France flew above the clouds. It was a clear day for a new adventure. It was a new beginning that scared me a little.

I took my bags and walked outside the airport after my arrival. Paris had looked the same as when my mother and I left it. There was a generation of new mimes performing on the streets. Locals and visitors who ate at the cafe were spectators of their display. I walked on the street my mother and I had toured years ago.

An old man's shop was where I would be staying until I got a flat of my own. I took a taxi to Monsieur Heberg's fish shop. He lived in a quiet town near the city. He rented out the studio above his shop to earn more money. Selling fish wasn't high on the market.

"*Bonjour, Mademoiselle*," he greeted me, waving his hat in front of him. He was an average man in his sixties. He had wavy gray hair that always stuck up when he

pulled off his hat. His blue eyes widened
to show off their crystal sea blue color.
The same eyes hid underneath his bushy
gray eyebrows. His face made me smile.
Monsieur Heberg was a former college
professor of philosophy, whom students
called Monsieur Berg.

"Every one of them was a hard knot
because they thought they knew more than
I, and they knew nothing. Even when I see
my former students today, they're unaware
of their lack of understanding." He paused
while he placed his index finger upon the
side of his chin. "Come on, I'll take you
to the cafe. A couple of the servers will
tell you all about philosophy, why it's
good to listen to Monsieur Berg and the
consequences if you don't. We can grab a
coffee and croissant. I'm sure you're a
bit famished after you're flight." He had
a dry sense of humor. He smoked
carelessly. "You just moved here from New
York, huh?"

"Yes, I lived in Switzerland before
and I have traveled around Europe."

Monsieur Berg stopped to look at me.
"There are no drugs here. I have a
philosophy about you hippies who travel
and wear those dull colors. You all are up
to no good."

"Monsieur Berg, that's not me. I
don't do drugs." Monsieur Berg put his two
fingers on my lips to silence me, speaking
in an agent's voice.

"My philosophy is that hippies never went completely away. They are now imposters, posing as world travelers. Searching the world for the best drugs and dope; you know, the term you freeloaders use. But there will be no dope here. My fish won't die an awful death such as that. I'm not someone who shares either," he revealed. His hand shook as he held it out for me to take. I wasn't sure to touch it or shake it. Still, I didn't want his first impression of me to be unpolite. I shook his hand consciously. My eyes didn't smile back. "I'm Bellina."

His eyes widened, "Bellina! Where are you from? I don't recognize your accent." It was all my years in Switzerland cut short and outgrown by New York. I was a mixed breed.

"I've lived in New York for a many years," I explained

"I see." Monsieur Berg looked down. "There's a cafe across the street. Would you like to go?"

"Yes." I couldn't wait to get to the café.

He grabbed his jacket. We left the shop. "Hold on." He went back in and turned the sign from open to *Be Back in 30 minutes*! "Don't worry. Everyone knows thirty minutes means an hour."

"What time is your shop open?" I asked.

"Eleven to four. I like to feed the fish fifteen minutes before ten so they

will look their best for the customers. I
give them a little chat before people come
in. The red fish becomes shy when company
comes and who needs a shy fish?"

We stopped in the middle of the road.
He looked at me. Then he looked away.

"Not I."

"Oh." We started back walking. I
figured I was going to meet some real
characters in Paris. The cafe was on a
corner. It had Christmas lights
surrounding it. We sat outside and waited
to be served.

"Ah, *Monsieur Berg comment-t-alle
vous?*" A young server filled our glasses
with water while saying hello to Monsieur
Berg. I thought he must have been a former
student of Monsieur Berg.

"Oh Knock it off. We both know you
can't speak French. So stop trying,"
Monsieur Berg snapped at the server. The
server rolled his eyes and then smirk a
smiled.

"Monsieur Berg, what may I get for
you?" His eye wandered to me, "*Bonjour*, I
see Monsieur Berg managed to get another
victim." He kept his eyes on me.

"Bellina," I said.

"Luc-Christian. Nice to meet you. I
hope you are able to tolerate Monsieur
Berg's unusual philosophy," Luc-Christian
smiled at me. His eyes were kind. They
were the same color blue as the ocean. He
had clean cut hair and his soft pink lips

made me blush. His smile showed off his perfect white teeth.

"Does the owner here pay you to flirt or work?" Monsieur Berg smirked.

"Monsieur Berg," Luc Christian began to respond back to him.

"Because I am ready to order, are you ready to take my order, server?" Monsieur Berg quickly cut Luc Christian off.

"I am, and I would love to know what you would like, Mademoiselle?" I smiled at him. I thought he and Monsieur Berg were acting like little boys, as soon as I had stopped laughing at my thoughts. Luc-Christian kept smiling at my silliness. I forgot all about the order.

"Where did you live before?" Luc-Christian asked me.

"Switzerland. Switzerland is my home. I-"

"Excuse me, but I didn't arrange a dating session for the two of you," Monsieur Berg interrupted Luc's and mine conversation, "And I am sick of waiting. I am not paying for a bare table and a dull conversation."

"I am sorry, Monsieur Berg. Hmm, Mademoiselle, what would you like?"

Monsieur Berg threw his hands up in disbelief, leaning back on his chair. I waved to Luc to serve Monsieur Berg first, but Luc continued with me.

"Mmhh, I guess I will have a cappuccino."

"A perfect baguette." His eyes pierced at mine.

"No, no, thank you," I said as I coughed out loud. He smiled shyly at me. I didn't smile back. I felt unsure about the attention. My face had shown my discomfort. My cheeks were hot like fire.

"Monsieur Berg, what may I get you now?"

"The manager," Monsieur Berg snapped at Luc. I watched them mock each other. I hoped once I owned my restaurant, my customers wouldn't be rude to me.

Luc said to Monsieur Berg, "I can have you kicked out of the cafe."

"I like to see you try," Monsieur Berg challenged.

"I would if you were here by yourself."

"Ha, let us be honest with each other. You simply cannot kick me or anyone else out of this cafe. You are powerless."

"I never felt more powerful now than ever!" Luc smiled at his cleverness.

"Shut your mouth and write this down, Luc. I want a double shot of espresso. Just bring out the cream for me."

"I'll be right out with your drinks." Luc grinned at Monsieur Berg. Luc's black hair matched his stunning eyes. When I wasn't too shy to pay attention to him, I saw his soft pink lips form into a beautiful smile. There was no doubt he was handsome. I had fallen in love with his sultry voice.

As Monsieur Berg rumbled on about poor service being the French way, I dazed off replaying the sound of Luc's voice. I saw him attending to many tables. Every time he looked my way. I quickly looked away, allowing my eyes the opportunity to read the writing on the wall.

Dear Mother,
I came as an early baby. A baby you could not keep. Away I went, into the hands the nurse felt fave, sailing blue rivers, walking along roads, driving distances that never seemed to end.
I thought of you along the way. One day I will find you on the bay.
Love your never forgotten
Sue

"That explains my philosophy on this subject." Monsieur Berg spoke of philosophy. His green eyes wandered off as he lit a cigarette. I watched him twitch his left eye. His hands began to shake. He looked like his mind was full of confusion he stood and slowly paced to the back. Not a word muttered from his mouth. I thought it was old age that made him wander off. Monsieur Berg always looked like he was looking for someone. I toned him out to think of how Sue was like me, a girl without her mother.

"I hope you are able to tolerate Monsieur Berg's usual sense of mentality." He flashed his million dollar smile at me.

His kind eyes held me in their capture for a while.

"I think I am just fine. Today is really my first day here. So, I'll see how the rest of my time goes with him."

"That is a super way to look at things." Luc-Christian sat down, "I was unable to handle him and all of his philosophy. That's why I outed in his class."

"And now he works here!" We jumped at the sound of Monsieur Berg's voice. He stood over us.

"Yes, lucky me. I had to transfer to a more suitable professor. This is just a get by job. Like your fish shop around the corner." Luc mocked Monsieur Berg. Monsieur Berg smirked back.

"No, this is what happens to all the students who fell out of my class. They're no longer inspired by my wisdom, and they fondle off into their own world of nothing."

"Monsieur Berg, you really shouldn't be so rude to people," I blurted out. I caught my words before I began the next sentence. I looked at Luc-Christian, then the wall. "He did nothing wrong to us."

"If I need advice, I will look it up!" he snapped at me.

I felt Luc's hand squeeze mine. He left to continue his work. Monsieur Berg and I finished our drinks. The hour was well up.

"You better get back to your shop," I reminded him.

"I never rush. This is my lunch, and whoever is at the shop can wait until I finish with it. Every now and then I need a long break." He covered his face with a newspaper. I thought what have I got myself into?

I wondered if I had time to find other housing options. It never paid to be cheap. After another hour, Monsieur Berg was ready to head back to his shop. Luc Christian came over to bicker with him one last time.

"I hope you two enjoyed your visit with us."

"I did, thank you," I politely told him.

"And, as always, Monsieur Berg is at a loss of words for a moment of time," Luc joked.

Before I could hear Monsieur Berg's response, I turned my attention back to the wall.

"I hope you and your mother meet one day on the bay, Sue," I whispered to the wall, softly kissing it. I kissed it to give Sue luck. Her letter reminded me of the letters I wrote to my mother, how one day instead of meeting at a bay, we will meet at a golden gate in the clouds above. When I stepped from the cafe, the clouds were the only thing I looked at. They were more than beautiful to me. I didn't start school for another two weeks. *L'Ecole de*

Culinaire had a reputation of being the top culinary institute in the world. The best of the best instructors in the culinary world taught there. The growing best of the best in the culinary world went there. I was accepted on a foreign student admission.

"Paris is going to be your new home," she told me.

Home! The home I came from was all lies. I had lived in many homes. All were lies except Ms. Hickens. My flat was next to the tower. The only reason I wanted to go up the tower was to scream at the top of my lungs. My empty flat helped me get the word *home* out of my head.

Two weeks was too long to spend it in my empty flat. I had to get out. It became time for me to build my life on my terms. The awakening of life with a moment of peace is what I sought. I stared out the only window of my flat. My flat was a simple large room.

There was a twin bed, a dresser, a nightstand, and a closet. Plain white walls stood at attention above my wood floors. Across the open floor was a stove, a small fridge, a counter with hot pads and a sink. I turned the water on, praying not to see brown water splashing out. Lucky, I thought. Clear water poured from the faucet down the sink. I left the faucet running.

I went to see the view from my window. A park with a fountain and petite

shops painted the picture for me. How
beautiful the world could be. The view was
breathtaking. It stole my heart and left
my spirits.

I spun around my flat. My arms flying
in the air, I spun more, knowing my walls
were watching the show. I ran to my light
switch to turn the lights on and off
several times. "I live here now!" I
screamed. I could make it anyway I liked.

I could design my studio to my
liking. Go, go, go; my feet didn't
hesitate to go. I ran outside. Night had
quickly fallen, something I didn't notice
when I looked out my window. But I loved
the natural light of the full moon, the
clouds that looked like balls of cotton
candy.

The whole scene had captured my
vision as the sky acted its own play. The
act consisted of animals, people, and what
my imagination desired. The clouds told a
story of a little girl whose balloon flew
away. She cried as her mother hugged her.
Her dog licked her leg. The dog stood on
his hind legs and the little girl hugged
him. I looked at story after story. The
clouds made a scene for the people in the
planes, a scene for the people looking up
from the streets.

That night I slept like an infant
dreaming of a bedtime story of a girl and
her dog.

Monsieur Berg was downstairs cleaning
a fish tank. "Good morning." I felt

cheerful and confident as I strolled around the shop.

"Shh." Monsieur Berg's finger covered his mouth. "Aahh, be a little more quiet. Do you want to wake the fish? They can hear everything." He spoke to me as if I had disturbed the whole shop. All the fish were swimming in their tanks. None were asleep.

"Good morning," I whispered low enough for him to hear me. He looked at me like I was the stupidest person he could run into. No matter on the look, I kept talking. "I know how important it is that you attend to your fish, so I'm going to shop for my studio."

I was about to close the shop's door when Monsieur Berg mumbled, "I would prefer if you stayed out all day. My fish don' like you as much as I thought they would, smarty." I watched him slowly search the shop. He looked from one glass to the next. "Where are you? On the days I really need you," he said. I knew his words were in no relation to me. He carried a lost feeling.

I hoped whomever he spoke to spoke back. I closed my eyes. I inhaled the fresh scent of the morning air. It filled my lungs, causing a burst of energy that kicked one foot in front of the other. Down the street I went with my outgoing, newly found, confidence. By next week I'll be fulfilling the goals I wanted to

achieve. At one time, it never occurred to
me I would ever be back in Paris.

I was glad I made it back to Paris. I
patted myself on the back. With one last
deep breath, I took off to explore the
streets of Paris. The petite shops left
its doors open for customers. Ms. Hickens
had given me enough money to buy furniture
and other things I may need to make Paris
my home.

Down the road was a design studio
that had pictures of room designs posted
outside. I stood in front of one design of
a classic, modern and glamorous, a
Fredrick de Croix, white leather sofa with
his signature area rug to match it. The
corners of the sofa were decorated with
blood orange throw pillows. A pecan brown
coffee table was in front of the sofa on
the signature rug. A dark wood vase of a
woman without a head was on top.

It had the newest entertainment
technology equipment to go in my living
room. A large frame glass separated the
living room from the work/study area. The
work/study area was a bold olive with a
cherry wood desk that had a library shelf
against the wall. There was a chair next
to the desk with a huge printed pillow on
the floor. A black and white photo of
zebras running in the jungle overlooked my
black and white room. The queen size bed
was white with black boards.

The bedroom walls were clear gray.
The dark red kitchen was the last section.

A black rectangular table that had three stools was in front of the kitchen. A green leaf plant was on the center of the table.

It was all so beautiful; it looked fearless. The drawing made me feel fearless. Walking away with pep in my step, I was on a mission to find furniture just like it.

Chapter 9

I was sure Monsieur Berg wouldn't mind my
painting the walls bold, inspiring colors.
I was ready to create my own Frederick de
Croix look. I walked into a small store
that looked like everything in the store
was of people's old junk. There were many
new, barely used materials to buy cheap. I
kind of felt exotic like a foreign shopper
lost in a store of usual things that may
not be there the next day.

Things you couldn't order nor remake;
only the usual things I would have to get
now or cry about it later. I overheard a
lady speaking with her girlfriend about
the French men and men in other cultures
and laughing at their dry humor. I
finished looking at all the stuff in the
store. I tore at the feeling of wanting to
spend the little budget I had with me.
When I didn't really know what I needed
for my studio.

Even though I had the thought of a
fearless woman in mind, my budget was fit
more for a lonely mouse. I left going from
one shop to the next. All the pretty
things I saw made me want to buy them. The
pastries in the windows were lovely to
look at. In France I believe it should be
illegal for anyone to eat the pastries
displayed in the window. A hand reached in

and took the cream puff of heaven right out of my eyesight. The blonde woman with her hair pulled back smiled at me. I did not smile back.

I felt like she robbed me of pressure. And that should be illegal. I found myself in front of a theater that had the most beautiful grand doors I ever saw. A young man stood out the door dressed like he was in front of a hotel entrance. He opened the door for a couple to enter. The smile on his face quickly vanished once the couple went inside. His smile came back once he saw me.

"Would you like to come in?" he asked.

"Yes, please." I walked to the beautiful doors. "May I touch the door, the gold trim?"

He laughed a little at me. "You may touch anything you like."

"*Merci*." Touch the gold trim on the beautiful door was what I did. The touch was not as soft and delicate as I had assumed it to be. The roughness explained the history of the doors. Doors trying to hold up their appearance to make sure people could not tell how old and rough it was. The door was like me. I paced back and forth in front of the door. We were lucky we found each other.

"Excuse me, Mademoiselle, the movie is about to start. Would you like to buy a ticket?" the young man asked.

"Yes, I would like to buy a ticket."
I didn't know what movie I paid the ticket
to see. I just figured it gave me
something to do. So I didn't care what I
saw. The inside of the theater was
magnificent.

All of Ms. Hickens' teachings about
the French Renaissance came to life in the
theater. The painting on the walls
captured all of the events I had learned
about. The lively art paid close attention
to all the details from textbooks. A long
hallway led people into the theater
showing the film. The chairs were grand,
with red valet and gold trimming.

The huge screen overshadowed the
room, making it impossible not to see it.
A few people walked in with their snacks
of popcorn, rice candy, and drinks. I paid
too much attention to the decor of the
theater. I did not see the concession
stand. To make this my favorite first
experience, I had to go to the concession
stand, at least to get a small box of
popcorn. Not to my surprise, the
concession stand looked like a mini cafe,
grand like the theater. I saw a black noir
film, *Countless in Couture*. I couldn't
fully understand it. I knew the characters
had found love in the middle of a 1930's
war. I didn't know what being a countless
had to do with it. I left the theater
feeling wonderful to continue my day. The
day stayed wonderful for me, too.

"Bellina, beautiful girl, please wait for me!" I turned around to see Luc racing to me, waving his hands. Once he caught up to me, he held his hand over his heart to catch his breath. "*Mon bella*, it's nice to see you again." He took off his hat. "You just come from the theater? How did you like it?"

"Hello, Luc," I couldn't help but laugh a little at him. He seemed like a little boy after a piece of candy. "I loved the theater. One day I'll come back to it. What are you doing here?"

"I got off work not too long ago. Would you like to take a walk with me?" He held out his hand in the gentlest way for me.

"Where are we walking to?" I asked.

"We will find our way," He informed me.

"Oh."

"Come on, walk with me." It seems when we were children, we were more spontaneous. When we grow older, we are more cautions. There isn't a middle; you are either spontaneous or you are cautious. I always thought, someone could not be too cautious.

"All you have to do is take my hand." Luc tried to convince me things would be alright.

"Okay." I walked past him without taking his hand. He put his hands inside his pockets and walked to my side. He leaned over so our arms would touch.

"How long is your stay in Paris?"

"Hopefully, until I graduate. After that I plan to go back to the states and work under a chef of a five star restaurant, hopefully!"

"Sounds like you have some doubts."

"I don't know if I would call it doubts. It's a big step to take. I want to get it right."

"I would say you know what you want. I am still figuring my life out and I'm not near close enough to tell people for sure what I want."

"Oh, I am still figuring out life myself."

"What makes you think that, beautiful?"

"My life has been a story of secrets. I have to figure all of this stuff out about what's true and what is not. I would rather deal with not knowing what in life I want to do versus not knowing the truth behind my existence."

Luc nudged my shoulder. At times I wished the secret I found stayed a secret. Knowledge will kill a person's soul; tear it apart and leave that person to put it back together again, all in the meantime becoming someone they never intended to be, all because of a secret they found that was not meant for them to find.

"I think confronting that secret you found is only going to make you a stronger person. Then you will be able to quit questioning your existence. In which,

lucky for me, you do exist. Because I
think I would still feel completely lost
if you didn't exist." I looked at him
looking down at me.

His eyes had capture mine. The
sunshine made the crystal sea blue color
of his eyes sparkle. He didn't look at me
in mischief, but sincerely. We walked a
little more. He nudged my shoulder.
"What's your favorite food, Bellina?"

"I love European cuisine. Romantic
cuisine that looks like you committed a
sin if you touch it."

"I know of the perfect place! You
will fall in love with it. You will more
so fall in love with the man taking you to
it." He smiled at me. He was handsome. A
slight breeze caught my eye, turning my
attention across the street.

There by a pond sat a boy sketching.
He sat alone, stalking people with his
eye. My smile faded as I admired him. He
was the most usual artist in a city that
created artists. There were many other
artists painting near him, but I could
tell he was a loner. Other artists stayed
out of his space.

"Come on, stop allowing little
distractions to get in the way of what you
are about to fall into with."

"What am I about to fall into with?"

"Love." He charmed a smile out of me.
He looked like a love struck puppy with
his hand held covering his heart. I
wondered if French men were struck at the

idea of being in love or if they really did fall in love. As for myself, I couldn't begin to share the foundation of love with anyone. The subject had never entered my mind in a realistic manner.

"Where are we going?"

"It's a surprise. You will like it."

"And if I don't?"

"You will. It suits your personality."

"Really, what's my personality to you?"

"Hmm, reserve, elegant, unique, and I believe you could be innovative, but I guess I will have to take more time to get to know you better."

"Perhaps you may even find me to be funny."

He pulled me in front of him. He was silent for a moment.

"No, you're not funny," he seriously said.

"I can be a little dorky-"

"No, I don't see it in you," he interrupted me. "Now let's get moving so we can get a table."

The Le Petite Café de Paris was the café Luc told me that fitted my personality. It reserved itself between two buildings. The inside natural colors spoke simple but elegant dining. The café towered like a pyramid, making it unique from the other cafes.

The menu had innovative cuisines only a true chef could master. The restaurant didn't seem like a place people could just walk into. It looked like a place where people had to reserve a seat at least two weeks in advance.

"How did you manage to get us a seat here?"

A huge smile appeared on Luc's face. "I have many talents. Getting seats to nice places is one of them."

"Thank you, but," I laughed at myself, "I feel a little out of place. I mean, I'm not properly dressed for this place."

"Who told you that?"

"What do you mean?"

"I mean what I said. Who told you you are not properly dressed for a place like this?"

"Look at me. I'm wearing jeans and a plain white shirt."

"You look great. You know, I think only you can put yourself in a category. And that's exactly what you are doing. Only the category you put yourself into is very negative," He viewed the menu.

"Sorry."

"Don't apologize; just make sure you stop categorizing yourself in a negative form."

I knew he was speaking the truth. I shouldn't allow myself to feel less, even if I don't look up to par.

"Do you know what you would like to start with?" He asked me, still viewing the menu.

    I didn't know what I wanted. I ended
getting a sandwich and café au lait.
    Luc and I continued our walk around
the city. The rest of the day was nice. I
liked the walk with Luc.
    The end of the week my studio was
still bare. The walls were left untouched.
The gift of cookware Ms. Hickens gave me
was still in its box. A single twin-size
bed played the role of furniture. I needed
to do something to bring my studio to
life.
    My studio should be vibrating in
color. It should have my life story
painted on it. It should be shown to all
who walk through my door. I had no idea if
there would ever be someone, but I was
opened minded. Cans of paint of valet red,
creamy vanilla, autumn orange, and prints
of leaves and roses were displayed.
    I took the day to figure out which
walls belong to what color. The kitchen
screamed for me to paint it red. The rest
of the studio asked for the creamy
vanilla. The bathroom begged for the
autumn orange. I got started painting. I
painted the entire studio in a day. It
didn't look professional; it looked like a
blind person's work. And sadly, a blind
person could probably do much better.
Still, the color made the studio look like
someone lived there.
    It will soon come together once I put
the print of leaves and flowers on the
walls. I painted the designs on sheets of

paper I was going to hang on the walls. I felt happy, like the feeling when one is filled with air and can fly. Only I wouldn't fly far away, just around my studio.

"Aawww, I smelled the paint downstairs. I hope, before you move, you'll paint it back to the white I had it." His sharp stare caught my attention. His face was pale. I couldn't figure if he was upset or not. "It looks nice."

"I will. I'm sorry, Monsieur Berg. I should have asked you first."

He waved his hand around. "It doesn't matter. This is your place now. It is, well, you are the first one to change it. The others were too scared to touch a thing in here. It looks good."

"Thank you, Monsieur Berg," I said happily.

"Where are you sleeping tonight?"

"What do you mean?" I was puzzled. Where else would I sleep?

"You cannot sleep here in all these paint fumes."

Now I was the pale one in the room. "Why?"

"My God, do they not teach students in America anything?"

"I was home school," I told him.

"Even worse. You're not supposed to be exposed to the lead in the paint. You can become brain dead or worse, stupid. You will stay with me tonight. Here, air out this place." He opened the window.

"Grabbed some stuff." He left my studio
door open. I grab as much as I could.

Becoming brain dead or stupid was
something I couldn't afford. I didn't know
how long before I started showing
symptoms. I had been painting in my studio
all day. My heart rushed at the thought of
becoming stupid. I saw my culinary career
vanish in front of my eyes.

Going from an executive chef to a
line cook wasn't what I had in mind. Get
out of here, get out of here, ran in my
mind. Within minutes I zoomed out of the
shop's door. Monsieur Berg's voice stopped
me from running farther with my bag in my
hands.

"What are you doing?" He had the same
look of confusion as I had on my face.
"Wow, can American girls be anymore?" He
didn't finish his statement. He looked at
me, squinted his eyes with the greatest
confusion on his face. He went inside, and
I stayed in the middle of the street
holding my things. My heart slowly
settled. I would only know what kind of
damage I caused myself later on. A few
moments later Monsieur Berg found himself
beside me.

"Next time don't run anywhere in a
panic. People see you're panicking and you
will be their next target. I do not want
to be the one to explain anything if
anything happens to you or anything else."

He walked ahead of me. "Come on, I
don't have all night."

"Here I come."

"Don't think men are the only one who prey. Women are predators, too. In knowledge, they are worse than men," he warned.

We arrived at a blue door, the door of the flat a couple of doors down from the fish shop. Monsieur Berg's flat had traces of a woman living in it. It was decorated in floras, cooking supplies were in the kitchen, and rosemary was in the center of candles. A photo of a beautiful blonde and a young Monsieur Berg hung above the candle.

"Monsieur Berg, do you remember your first kiss?" From the way the sparkle shined in her eyes, I could tell he was hers. Monsieur Berg hesitated, sitting on his arm chair.

"I do remember." He looked down at his shoes. "I was fifteen; fifteen with pimples covering my face. I didn't think any girl would ever be interested in me." He relaxed his shoulders, shyly smiling. "I was fifteen. The girl of my dreams stood in front of me. I took her by her shoulders and kissed her for a very long time. When I finished, I stood back and waited for her to slap me. I was so scared, that she was going to do it, but she lost the mortified look on her face, grabbed my collar, pulled me to her, and kissed me like I was the last man she was ever going to see."

The photo of him and the young blonde stared back at him. "Heidi. She was German. Her family moved here to escape the war; little did they know they moved right into it. She was beautiful, like a perfect picture. I could just dream about her all day. Two years after that kiss, we married.

I enlisted in the military and was sent to war. I received many letters from her. We wrote all the time, or at least I tried to. Until one day the letters stopped. At first I thought it was because mail could not reach the area I was posted at. That post was blown by the Germans. The men I was there with kind of got stuck there. We were not allowed to move out because the enemy was still close by. I thought Heidi and I were going to be together forever.

My greatest fear was Heidi could not take not hearing from me and eventually leave me for another man. That fear became my greatest wish now." He had tears forming in his eyes. "I could deal with that fear versus to my findings after years of being home. No sign of her was anywhere when I came home two years later. I didn't search for her.

I closed my eyes and wished her the best. The best was to let her go to be happy. Every beautiful girl deserves to be happy. Five years later, after having plenty of rendezvous with various women, my house burned down. The whole time I had been back I didn't bother to move or touch anything in the house. Nor did I have the will to find anything.

I never allowed any woman in the house. You are the first one since my wife. I would always go to the woman's house. Sometimes I would leave running in my shorts because her husband would show up. I guess I was still holding out for her in case she came walking through that door. After I removed all of the debris and ash from the house, I found all of my letters that I wrote to her. She read them and stamped the unfinished letters she was going to send to me. I thought, my poor baby. I sat there as the sun disappeared, the clouds creeped in and the rain fell down. I reread the letters.

Not one letter ever spoke of her being lonely or upset at me for leaving her. She understood and said she would wait however long it took for me to return to her. Freeing the people from this evil war was the only importance. In her last letter she had become sick. Smallpox had taken over her petite body. She felt she couldn't fight it anymore.

I went to the library during that time. I spent most of my time there studying the file drawer that held death certificates. One day I opened the drawer and found hers. I started asking around and found out her family had moved back to Germany and that is where she was buried.

I was more broke getting out of the military then, from when I went in.

I have never been to her grave. But every day I hear her from when she closed her eyes to speak to me. Every morning I make sure she hears me, too." Monsieur Berg talked the whole time, staring at Heidi. Tears were still in his eyes; none had fallen. "The best time of my life started with a kiss." His story ended. I started to ask more questions, but I didn't want to interrupt his moment. He closed his eyes, and I knew they were speaking to each other. Monsieur Berg was not an old bag. He just missed his first love. Missing first loves can make one go crazy, putting them in a lonely place. I went to sleep in the next room. I heard Monsieur Berg breathing throughout the night. Something told me he and Heidi fell asleep together.

* * *

"Hello, honey, I have missed you so much. It's not the same without you here," Ms. Hickens' sweet voice comforted me.

"I missed you, too. More than you may know. How are things there?"

"Things are good. I started a job working at the high school. I needed to get out of the house." A jealous feeling erupted in me. She was with other kids who were near my age. They were taking her time. Soon she would forget about me.

"Why are you teaching?"

"Bellina, hun, what's the matter?"

"Nothing is the matter with me." I listened to her breathing. I could tell she didn't know what to say. "Does teaching make it easier to forget about me? I mean, are you trying to replace me?"

"Oh, honey, no way. No one can replace you. I simply think you are unforgettable. Oh, honey, is that how you feel?"

"Yes, I do."

"I am sorry. I love you. I am proud of you for going all the way over there. That takes bravery to follow your dreams. I would like to share that bravery with another young person. I pulled all the inspiration you gave me to put it in someone who needs it."

That never rang a bell to me. It was her nature to help people. That's why her God made her.

"Please forgive me for being selfish."

"That's fine. It happens to all of us sooner or later. Honey, no one will ever take your place. Now start telling me about Paris."

"It is wonderful. I love it very much. The clowns still joke in all the towns, people still dance in streets, and the artists still paint on the bench." The lone painter came to mind.

"That sounds like a heavenly place."

"It is! The sweets are so beautiful; it is a sin to eat. They taste like a delightful sin."

"One day I plan to meet you there."

"Yes, when are you coming?" My excitement made me jump.

"First, let me plan it." She said laughing.

"That would help me, to see you. Then I won't feel alone like I do now."

Her laughter stopped, "Honey?"

"Yes, Ms. Hickens?"

"You are never alone."

We kissed over the phone and hung up. My day was starting as hers was ending. The final design of my studio became everything I had imagined it to be. I had my urban chic in autumn colors. I threw out the bed and bought an ivory sofa bed.

The middle of a cherry wood coffee table pulled out into side chairs. All my clothes went into my walk-in closet. My things were unpacked. Ms. Hickens taught me preparation. I laid out my clothes for the week. My classes started this week. I eventfully laid on my sofa to rest. I counted the purple dots on the ceiling that swirled above me.

"Bellina, Bellina." The knock on the door made me jump. "Bellina, it's me, Luc," Luc chanted.

I opened the door to a boutique of pink roses.

"These are for you." The roses moved closer to me, revealing Luc's flirty smile.

"Thank you." Surprised to find him at my door with roses, I took them, unaware of his next gesture. The moment had stopped abruptly. I realized what happened soon after. No one had ever kissed me other than my father and my mum. The kiss reminded me of the Jane Hobburt movie I saw with Ms. Hickens, soft like a feather and light like air.

I passed my time to slap him for the rudeness of his spontaneous act. Slapping was something Jane would do. She only had to slap her leading man once to bring tears to his eyes. I kind of like the unexpected kiss, but didn't want to show I did. I put my hand up to signal stop.

"Do not ever do that again!" my voice roared. Luc took a step back.

"Pardon me. You are so beautiful, that I couldn't resist stealing a kiss." I put my hand down and started pacing off.

"Wait up, I said I'm sorry. What more would you like me to say?"

"Nothing more, let's just walk." We walked in silence. We were mute, listening to the sounds of the people and the earth around us. Lilies fell from the sky as I wished to catch them. I thought if it rained how lovely it would have been with the lilies falling from the sky. I tilted my head back. I felt Luc's eyes on me. It didn't matter I was off in a different world.

It was the story of love that makes love wanted. A person can pull and pull. If the other person doesn't pull back, then the story will have a tragedy. The person never pulling back allowed the story never to begin. Love would stay a draft of outlines and synopsis.

Luc slipped me his hand to hold. Since he brought me the roses, I thought to be kind and take them. I thought he was handsome. I didn't feel like ending the story with him. In the middle of my endless thoughts, the painter, whom I barely saw before, sat not far away from where Luc and I were walking. I knew it was him.

He wore the same clothes from the first day I saw him in, black slacks, a white button-down blouse, black flip flops, and blue jean jacket lying over his lap as he worked on his random masterpiece. Again I couldn't see his face. He seemed like nothing was present, only him. He looked up for a split second and back down again. Not even his art muse was present.

How lucky he could space everyone out. I never could do that because I was always the center of the circle while everything else raced around me. It was the same loneliness, only in different forms. The lone painter with the hidden face proved to me that my story had yet to be more than an outline. Luc had squeezed my hand.

"Ouch." I yanked my hand back.

"Oh, I'm sorry. I had no idea of my strength. Please forgive, beautiful." He begged for my forgiveness. Both my hands went up into the air.

"I forgive you. My hands are tender," I told him.

"Then I will have to handle them with care." He was sincere with every word from his mouth.

The protective tone in his voice stayed with me the whole night. He wrapped his coat around my shoulders. We continued on until he took me back to my studio.

* * *

It had been two days later since Luc and I were together. I didn't remember much of that night. I remembered the feeling I had when I saw the lone painter, sitting and painting. I got up to take a shower.

Luc was working when I went to the café. His boss was giving a lecture to a new employee. He pointed to an estranged couple.

"Hello, *mon bella*. It's nice to see you." Luc came behind me, kissing me on my cheek. "I'm sorry, I cannot help myself."

"It's okay. *Merci*," I told him as I smiled back. "What's your boss giving a lecture about?"

"Come, sit with me." We sat at table that was by our side. "See, they are tourists. See the way they're sitting? Reserved; see how her purse is wrapped around her arm and guarded on her lap and him, he's hunched over like he's about to fall into the empty bowl in front of him. Those tourists I can tell them how much to order, what is what, if they do not like it, they can leave. I am not pushy nor am I charming. See the two women with their poodles?"

"Yes, I see them," I told him.

"They are French, they know what they want. I do not have to be so rough."

"What do you mean?" I asked.

"I spend less time with them. With the tourists, they try to keep me the

whole time they are here. That is what
he's explaining to the new guy. Do not
waste time with anyone."

"Oh, *mais*, isn't it taking the time
and charming the guest that keeps them
coming for more?"

"*Oui, mais,* this cafe doesn't work
that way. Plus, I think only women servers
are charmers."

"Oh, really. I know some men who are
charmers, too."

Luc laughed. "Name one."

"Luc Christian." And he was charming.
I smiled at him. "Well, I think you should
start charming more." I slipped a euro
into his hand.

"Maybe that's what I will start
doing." He smiled back.

"Luc, I need you inside, *vient*,
vient!" A thin man waved Luc over.

"Work calls for me. You are welcome
to stay. I will bring you something to
eat."

"I think I will stay for a while."

"Wonderful, I feel like a lucky man
today."

"That is great!" I had a big smile.
"Why do you feel so lucky? What's going to
happen for you?"

Luc looked at me with a smile and a
sparkle in his eye. He never answered my
question. I figured he was still waiting
for an answer himself. He left blowing
kisses at me. The gesture made me smile. I
didn't mind his charm; it made me feel

good knowing he went out of his way to make me smile.

I sat there for a couple of hours watching Luc hustle through work. He was able to bring me a cup of coffee and puff cream pastry. Four days before I was supposed to meet with my guidance counselor, Luc and I spent every second together. He was at my door before I made it out of bed. Breakfast first thing in the morning was his favorite time.

"An hour of nothing to do but eat and chat is the time of my life. Now I have you to share it with." He would eat a muffin as I wondered if it was appropriate for him to be over while I was still dressed for bed. We spoke of politics, his favorite topic. "Vincent Dupre should be the President of France. He's the new Republic. I believe he will bring order to all of France." Luc spoiled our breakfast with his nonstop politics discussion. "Listen to me, my studio is not your political ground discussion flat! Go march through the streets and rant all you want. You will not rant here!"

Luc mocked me, "Feisty one, are you? I love politics. If you really want to know someone, get to know them through politics."

"Luc, I'm going to ask you to leave now. You again have waked me up and ruined my breakfast! While you're walking to wherever you're headed to, think about how your politics got you kicked out of my studio!"

He was hysterical. "Alright, I'll leave. You may keep the breakfast I bought you." He got up and went to the door. "Just do one favor for me."

"What is that?"

"Think about that your attitude is the exact reason why men don't like women in politics."

Bam! The nearest object I could throw at the Luc was a vase I didn't want. He slammed the door shut before it hit him. I had enough with the politics of the world, mostly because politics failed me a while ago.

Chapter 10

Fall semester started on a Monday. Late
arrivals had to meet with an admission
counselor for a decision about their
agenda and the classes they were going to
take. My counselor was trained to counsel
the foreign students from America. Kate
Benning moved to Paris after eight years
as an executive chef at a four star
restaurant in Spain.
Originally she was from New Jersey. She
had bleached blonde hair that fitted her
tan skin. She wore glasses to match her
crisp, black, tailor skirt suit.

        "Hello, Bellina." Madame Benning had
a high pitched voice. I sat in front of
her. Her many certificates of awards were
plaster on the walls. "Most of our
students from American come when they want
to get an advanced degree in the culinary
field. It's always nice to have a young
adult enroll in our school. It shows you
have a drive to succeed and want to take
your career further in life. In your
application I read you haven't received
any formal training. You learned from
home."

        "Yes, I did learn from home. I assure
you I'm a great cook." I sat straight in
my chair. The tone in my voice became
mature as I spoke to Madame Benning.

"Of course you are, otherwise you wouldn't be here. The world's top chefs learned from their mothers kitchens. They took an aggressive approach to what their mother's taught them and that has opened doors for you to be sitting in front of me today." Her voice deepened as much as a high pitch sound could. "Your counselor throughout your time here will be Madame Cortez. She is amazing. You will meet with her tomorrow. Now she'll answer all the questions you have about classes. Bellina, it is wonderful to have you here at our school." She smiled at me.

"Thank you for having me," I said with a smile.

"If you need to apply for more financial assistance, you may do so before the end of this term. Changing housing arrangements is done through me. I asked you to make an appointment about two months in advance to change your housing."

"Okay."

"I guess we are done if you do not have anything for me to answer or go over with you."

"No, I do not."

"It is nice meeting you and, again, come see me if you need anything."

"Thank you, goodbye."

I left her office waiting for tomorrow and the day after. I wanted to begin now. I knew what I was getting into. I had no questions or concerns. I just wanted to cook.

It was a rainy day as I stared at her sitting in front of me. She pushed papers around her desk. The papers were shuffled, overlapping each other. A small bronze plaque with her name printed on it stared right at me. I stared back. Madame Cortez was an American from Chicago. Marriage relocated her to Paris. She would be my counselor during my time at the institute. She counseled forty students and twenty students independently.

"I'm always on a go. I've never had a student who never had a problem." She shuffled through her papers some more, looking up to make sure I was still in the room with her.

"Just give me one second and I'll be able to give you your time."

My time is what she said. I was looking forward to it, too; time where I only had to talk about me. It has been a long time since I had to talk about me. It may have been selfish to think only about me, but if I didn't think about me, then who would? I didn't want to leave Madame Cortez with the whole job of thinking of me. I needed to take some credit, too, and that I did. I waited patiently for her to finish.

"I'm sorry about this. I did not realize how unorganized I was until the last minute. Don't follow my lead on your first day. Your whole time here will quickly fall off track if you do."

Believe me, I won't!" It sounded much better in my head than said out loud. Madame Cortez quirked a smile.

"I'm glad you will be taking your time here, serious."

"Yes, I plan to," I insisted.

"What do you plan to get out of your time here?"

"I plan to become advanced in my career and network with others. Creating art through food is my passion, plus I love to cook."

"That's a great attitude you have. How long have you known you wanted to be in the culinary field?"

"It was my first thought of a career. Ms. Hickens introduced me to it when we were exploring other countries."

"Your Ms. Hickens?" She had a puzzled look on her face.

"I call her mine. She pretty much raised me."

She nodded as if she understood. "How do you like Paris?"

"I've always loved Paris!"

"Sounds like you're in the right place then."

I nodded. I was in a great place.

"Here at the *L'Ecole de Culinaire* we take pride in the quality of skills we instill in our students. As you know, many of our alumni have gone on to run five star restaurants. Some have cooked for royals of many countries. Several students have their own cooking shows. We have many students who have stayed to teach the up and coming culinary professionals. I can't stress enough how proud these students make me to be a part of this institute. You will find all of the support you need here. Here at *L'Ecole de Culinaire*, we pay close attention to technical and artistic details. The top student is the executive chef for the entire year."

My heart did not skip; it leaped back and forth. It leaped as if it was going to explode from my chest and land on Madame Cortez's desk. I wanted to be the executive chef. A whole year of being head chef was what I was going to strive for. No other person wanted it more than I. I knew it in my heart. This was what I was meant to do. A rejoiced song threw my spirits up. The song trapped and deposed any doubts I once had. My feet lost gravity. A new world had begun for me. I wanted to know every class I needed to take to make it as the chef. I wanted to know every spice, every scent, every herb, and every taste. My eyes were open now, wide open.

"That's what I want."

"Pardon me, Bellina?"

"That's what I want. I want to be the executive chef. It's my calling. It's why I came all the way here, to be the top chef."

She saw the tears in my eyes. They were tears of joy.

"Then that's what we will make you."

"Thank you." The huge lump in my throat barely allowed me to speak. Yes it was love I found, and it was Paris who bought it to me. For that I'll be forever grateful.

It was overwhelming how many people it took to run a restaurant, all of them following my lead, listening to my every word.

"Station one I need a shallot over risotto for table four. These are tapas; in other words, make the plates small."

"Yes, chef!" They would shout back. Orders would follow left and right after that. I'll be in pure heaven, loving every minute of it. Paris is the city of love. It had introduced me to it. I left with my schedule in hand.

I was to start tomorrow bright and early. Outside still looked cold. I didn't care; in the rain, shine, below temperature, desert dry heat, I still could prepare the best meal anyone would ever taste. Why, the knowledge was simple; cooking was what I was born to do.

I thought of my luck on getting here. I wondered how many people on the street got a chance at luck. What did they do with it? The school was a twenty minute walk from my flat. It was plenty of time for me to daydream.

"There you are. That little boy came over for you. I told him to wait in your room. I didn't want to be bothered with him." Monsieur Berg's voice daunted the place. His shop became dark and gloomy when he spoke in his hostile tone.

"Luc is here!" I was somewhat excited to see Luc. I wanted to share my day with him. I rushed upstairs, fading out Monsieur Berg's words.

"Luc." I burst in the door.

"Hello, beautiful." Before I knew it, we were in each other's arms. He kissed me and the things I had to say left my tongue. "What? What is it?" he asked

"You just catch me off guard when you do that to me."

"Do what? Kiss you?"

"Yes, it makes me feel uncomfortable."

"How come you don't like it when I kiss you? You flew into my arms as if you were dying to see me than you reject me."

"I'm not rejecting you. I just don't want you to kiss me."

"I should be allowed to kiss you. That's what people do."

I sat on my sofa. "I was excited to tell you how my day went. I start school tomorrow. They have this program that if you're the top student, you can be the executive chef for your whole last year at the school."

"I know about it," Luc commented bluntly. He was more interested in receiving kisses from me. "I want, I want." He stopped what he was saying. "I know we're only known each other for a couple of weeks. I know how I feel about

you. I like you. I like our time together
and want more time together. I mean, we
don't have to rush anything. Let's see
where this can go with us."

I did like Luc. Any girl would be out
of her mind not to. I was scared of the
truth. The truth changed me. I didn't want
it to change Luc's feelings toward me.

"You don't speak about your parents.
Why not?"

It was the truth no one should hear.
I wasn't ready to accept. I looked at him.
He waited for an answer; an answer I never
wanted reveal to him.

"It's okay. When you're ready to
share with me whatever it is that took
over the look on your face, I'll be
willing to listen."

I felt relieved of not having to go
down memory lane.

"Let's start this whole day over."

"What do you mean?" I asked him.

"Go to the door and bust in like you
did before. We're going to have a retake."

I laughed at Luc's silliness, but
thought the retake would be best to do.
Once again I ran in and was greeted by
Luc. A huge smile hung on his face.

"Hello, Beautiful."

He took a knee and took my hand. He
slowly kissed it. I felt his breath,
breathing on my skin. I liked the kiss.

"My classes start tomorrow." He led
me to my sofa.

"Congratulations to you. When you finish school, hopefully there'll be a reason for you to stay in Paris. Paris is always looking for a few great chefs."

I refused to look at his eyes for fear of them swallowing me up. He wanted to be my reason to stay. That I knew.

"How did your day go?"

"My day is going better. It was down a few minutes ago, but it picked back up." We laughed a little. "May I hold you?" he asked me. "That's fine." We sat still for a moment.

"You have to lean back into my arms."

"Oh!"

"Like this." Luc directed me into his arms. My back was as solid as a rock. After a moment, the position just felt awkward. My neck hung off the side of the sofa as my feet flew into the air. I didn't like someone holding me.

"I can't be like this. I have to be comfortable and ready for my class tomorrow. This is hurting my neck," I said.

Luc pulled me up. "Sorry. Maybe we should sit like this." He started to pull me into another position.

"Luc, no," I said, "Let's just sit the way we are."

Luc let out a deep breath. "I'm fine with that."

"I'm sorry. This is all new to me."

"You don't have to apologize. There's nothing to feel sorry about. When the time is right, one day you will be able to relax in my arms," he softly said.

I wished that one day was today. I wanted to know what was wrong with me. A prefect man was sitting next to me. He wants to love me and I'm unsure about receiving his love.

"I may be entering school for business."

"That'll be great. What made you think of doing that?" I asked.

"So when you graduate and decide to stay here, you can be the executive chef in my restaurant." Luc's tone of voice never changed. It was the same tone as the day I met him.

* * *

Tuesday morning finally came. The day was different. The climate shifted gears. The sun beamed on Luc's face. He'd stayed the night, sleeping on the floor next to my pull-out sofa. I couldn't tell whether it was my excitement or Luc's breathing that kept me up all night. Regardless, my sleepless night wouldn't affect my day.

"May I walk with you?" His puppy eyes watched me grab my jacket.

"Yes, I'll like that."

He held my door open for me. We walk past Monsieur Berg, as he counted his

morning accounts. Luc led us out of the
fish shop. I smelled the fresh air. Summer
was long behind us. Autumn was here to
stay for a while. I didn't mind because
autumn was my favorite season.

"How did you sleep last night?" I
asked him.

"I slept like a baby." He smiled at
me. "I slept well."

"You slept well on the floor?"
Suspense rose in my voice.

"Yes, I did. I was fortunate to be
cast away in my dreams. The floor didn't
bother me."

"What dreams casted you away?" I had
to know.

"You, You were the dream that casted
me away." He looked straight ahead. "Do we
have time to stop for a small breakfast?"

"How small of a breakfast?"

"The crepes stand, right there. We
can grab one and eat it on the way."

We ate our crepes at a nearby table.

"Luc, I have to go! I can't be late."
I got up and started to run. Time wasn't
on my side.

"Slow down. Come on, we'll get you
there." He ran behind me, leaving our
unfinished crepes on the table.

I had made it right on time. The
school was much bigger than I had
recalled.

"Thank you for the breakfast," I told
him.

"You're welcome."

"Have a good rest of the day."

"I will, and you do the same." He kissed my cheek. I smiled back at him, giving him a hug. "Now go," he insisted. I knew Luc stood looking at my back fading farther away.

I found the classroom without any problems. The room wasn't an ordinary classroom.

It was model as an open kitchen. Five tables with stools were on the opposite side of the kitchen. The tables were made of wood. There was a stove on top of it. The ovens were on the other side of the room. Like any other kitchen, pots and pans were visible everywhere around the room.

Knives and utensils were sharp and placed not too far from our reach. Our white aprons hung on coat racks. Baskets of fruits, vegetables, and some dairy products were on the tables in front of us. Nutrition facts decorated the wall. It was a professional workplace.

The noise grew louder as the other students found the way in. They all took their seats at one of the stools. Besides myself, there was one other girl in the room. She didn't look at me. The rest of the students were white men. None of them spoke to me or her. I realized getting to the top was going to be a lonely road.

My goals I wanted to achieve weren't out of reach. My goal began on the day I arrived in Paris. Ms. Hickens had always

told me, never step down and allow someone
else to step in my place. Friends or no
friends; becoming the executive chef was
my main focus.

"Good morning, *bonjour*, *bonjouro*,
Hello. I'm Monsieur Tompee and this is
Introduction to Nutrition. It's a
celebration of the food that looks,
tastes, and makes you feel good." He went
to his desk, opened the drawer, and tossed
apples to the rest of the classroom.

He adjusted his glasses as he reached
for an apple. Monsieur Toupee was
attractive. He dressed causal, his black
hair was clean cut with gray highlights
and his green eyes saw everyone in the
class."

I sat back and wondered if a woman
had ever run the school's restaurant.
Maybe I'll be the first woman to do so.
Monsieur Toupee continued to talk,
explaining the class in detail.

I didn't have a break between the two
classes. The class of *Introduction into
the Mixture of Spices* hadn't let out yet.
I was able to peek into the doors of other
classes nearby. They all were designed the
same. I wandered a little farther down the
hall. At the end of the hall, signs guided
people to the school's restaurant. I went
out following the signs to the restaurant.
I just wanted to peek at it.

People started walking into the
restaurant. I was excited. The restaurant
had fit my image of it and much more.

Locals and students filled the restaurant. I couldn't wait to be there as the executive chef.

If a student wasn't at least the sous chef, they were servers. I only had my eye on being the top chef. The students didn't clean the restaurant; hired help was meant to do that. I was more than determined to be the executive chef. On my way back to class, my mind fast-forwarded to me calling orders and tasting plates of food before they went out.

I was wearing my white chef's jacket. I didn't want to wear the chef's hat because I was too intense in cooking the food. Working without a hat would be fine, I thought. Some of the students were leaving the classroom when I returned. While the new students came into the classroom, the professor put three small glasses in front of each empty chair. He remained silent. We all found a seat and waited for the professor to speak.

"Welcome to my class. I'm sure you all have heard that all day. We all mean it when we say it. I'm Monsieur Seukia. I began my career cooking in kitchens of the houses my mum cleaned. Now I'm teaching you here." Monsieur Seukia had smooth dark skin. His head was bald. His brown eyes were big. He was muscular built. He had a French accent.

"I want you to form a group and do the same for the pepper you all did for the salt. I want two groups. Discuss what the pepper taste like to each of you and we'll discuss it when you're finished."

All of them stood to form their own group. I looked for one to join. The circle closest to me was closed off from me squeezing into, leaving me to go to the other group. They all looked at me in a dirty way. I went back to the other group and stood in the back with a small glass of pepper in my hand.

I raised my mouth out with the bottle water to rid the salt and breakfast taste, then I closed my eyes to taste the pepper while the boys talked. I blocked everyone from my thoughts. The pepper took center stage. For a second I forgot about the rudeness the men had shown me. I escaped to pure heated heaven.

The pepper didn't cause a fire in my month; it took me to a nice hot sand beach. I tasted all of the flavors and thought of new flavors to create from it. I opened my eyes. "Excuse me." I reached over one of the men to set my glass down. "The flavor I got …"

"I guess we're done!" A brown-haired boy cut me off and stood in front of me. "Let's return to our area and wait for the other group to finish."

The group dismissed without me. I stood with my mouth still open, ready to talk. They all went back to their seats. I stood there trying to figure out why I being treated like I was invisible.

No matter how much I wanted it, I would never treat them in such a way.

After the class ended, I remained seated. "Monsieur Seukia, have I done something to offend anyone?"

He started to arrange two new small glasses of species for his next class, not paying any attention to me. Then he stopped in front of me.

"Bellina, isn't it?"

"Yes." My voice deepened.

He took a breath. Never did he make eye contact with me.

"This's not a profession for a woman. You should be in child development. That is a profession women excel in not outside of childhood. Look, what did you see in my classroom?"

"Nothing I hadn't seen before." I was going to tell him I saw tables, posters, and tools to make a kitchen. I had a feeling that wasn't the answer he was looking for, so I decided against saying it. Seeing the tables and the things that made up a kitchen was the typical answer he was waiting to hear.

"Men," his voice roared with pride. I understood I was the only woman in the class, but the men weren't as smart as I was. I roared my voice back at the professor.

"Yes, but they couldn't provide you with the answers you were searching for. Yes, me, a woman, did. I've never been around children, but food I've been

around, and you or the other men are not
going to stop me from becoming executive
chef. No matter how much you ignore me." I
had considered maintaining self-control.
After the treatment I received from my
fellow classmates and instructors today,
maintaining self-control was far from my
mind. I wanted respect. I wanted it now.

"Listen to you." His voice was
calmer. "Do you really want to go your
whole culinary career being ignored? Why
would anyone go through that?"

"Because I want it more than anyone,
here; I'm not here for them." I was almost
screaming at him, becoming more upset,
"and I'm over here. Not over there, not
the wall or the board!" Finally he looked
at me. We were both silent.

"You get what you ask for, Bellina.
If I were you, I would think about the
things I want."

"I have and this is it."

He nodded but disagreed, "Then you
are in for some major disappointments."

I took that as my cue to leave.

"Thank you and have a good day." No
matter how he felt about my being at the
school, I was still polite. Ms. Hickens
would have a stroke if she found out I
wasn't. She hated rude people. I wondered
how far a person should be polite to
someone if it's not returned.

"Just be polite," she would always
say. I left the classroom and made it
outside. I walked with my notes in my

hands and pens stuck behind my ears. I was too angry to cry and too weak to stay mad.

"Hey, how was your first day?" He held out his arms for me. I sat beside him and allowed him to wrap them around me.

"I liked my first class; the second, it may take a while for me to fit in."

"Ah, don't fit in, you will be like the rest of them."

"Were you here the whole time?"

"No," Luc said, laughing. "I left and actually just made it here before you were released."

"Oh."

"Why, now you don't think I'm romantic anymore?"

"Ha, ha," I said smiling at the gray clouds. They were going to stay gray all day. "Thank you for coming back." After my last class I didn't expect to see Luc, but was more than glad to see him. Since he worked at a cafe, talking to him about my day would be easy. He understood.

"It gets worse before it gets better. However, you're not going to have to go through those worst times alone." It started to drip raindrops. They dripped as we stayed sitting on the bench.

"Where did you go?" I asked him.

"I went to apply for spring classes," he said proudly.

"In what?" I asked.

"Political Science. I love politics, and I'm good at it."

"How are you good at it?"

"I'm good at putting up a fight. All politics is putting up a fight. A person can change the world by putting up a fight for their beliefs," he campaigned.

"Why would you have to learn how to fight when you can fight for free on the street?"

"It's not that simple. Fight on the streets is what thugs do. I'm talking about fighting with your voice. Your voice is more powerful than your fist, because your fist leaves one punch. You hold your arm that hurts for a while until you feel no more pain from it.

You say ouch, then move on. Now words cause more than an ouch! They make people change their ways. Words stick in people's heads forever. The right words can change a nation. The right words can keep someone alive. The wrong words can do the opposite. That's what I want, to say those right words that change a nation."

The raindrops began to soak my notes. Luc kept holding me silently. I thought he was thinking of his battle of words and how he could change the world. Luc's heart spoke about changing the world. Silently I cheered for him. I wanted him to be the voice of the people who couldn't fight. I wanted him to make the world better. For it had changed me. I caught Luc staring down at the ground. I felt someone else should be sitting in his arms, not me.

"Sorry," he whispered into my ear, then kissed me twice on my cheek. "Are you ready to go, love?"

"Yes, I am." We helped each other up. We left hand in hand, walking in the raindrops. "At first I wasn't for sure about studying political science but my father reassured me, I was suited for it. He studied medicine, though his passion was for politics. I was the son who was going to carry out his love. His love had eventfully become my love. I always thought how strange, his love developed on me. I could never find anything else I wanted to do."

"I know how you feel. Nothing stuck to me except cooking. I decided long ago cooking was what I was meant to do. Sometimes I think cooking chose me."

And it did. I watched the performer pull my name out of his many hats pairing it with cuisine. He knew my destiny. I focused on the big picture, achieving my dream.

In class I was like a cheetah. I was fast, efficient, first to be done with my work. I excelled in food preparation and baking. Excelling was good, but I wanted to master the art of it all. I figured that was the only way I was going to get to the top.

Chapter 11

Time flew by faster than I could blink an
eye. It was my third year and I was the
head of the class. Some students formed
friends. I mostly stuck to myself. Luc
Christian was my only real conversation at
the end of the day until I kicked him out
for his continuing talks of politics.
    "I love you more and more each day,"
he told me. His eyes lit when he said it.
    "What makes you so sure you love me?"
    He held my hand tightly. "One day
I'll prove it to you," he said. I didn't
know how he was going to prove it. It was
far from my mind. I enjoyed the time we
spent together. Our time together kept my
mind off a lot of things. I still had to
prove myself to be at the head of the
class.
    Every year there were new faces I
was paired up with. The culinary
instructors seem to get worse by the year.
There was less instruction and more risk-
taking. The third year counted the most.
It decided who would run the restaurant.
We were encouraged to take summer cooking
classes at the school or restaurants. I
signed on for the summer classes at the
school. I was determined to get ahead. I
was determined to be first. The summer
took a toll for everyone.

Monsieur Berg seemed to have a loss for words. His world had stopped as he waited for his departure to be with his wife. I came in the door each day to Monsieur Berg sitting in his chair behind the cash register, staring into space. The fish swam back and forth; he never noticed me feeding them.

Then again, he never noticed anything anymore. Monsieur Berg's jokes stopped, and he kept his smart remarks to himself. He held on to the black and white photo of his young wife. I knew she was talking to him, telling him to 'to have a little patience, I'll be ready for you soon.' He was waiting to say, 'I am ready.' Until then I found it to be my priority to keep his spirits up.

"Today is Tuesday, Monsieur Berg," I told him. The outside changed its scenery as with the weather. "Today is Saturday, Monsieur Berg." Soon Monsieur Berg began being lifeless at his own home. I figured he needed some time to himself.

* * *

I turned my studio into a mini bistro and bedroom. I started experimenting with new cuisine and spices. "Welcome to Bellina's Café," I greeted Luc at the door.

"*Salut,* glad to see you're having a cheerful day."

"Come in, I've made something special for you."

"It smells like you put your heart in the pot you were cooking for me."

I looked at Luc, "You're going to love what I've made."

"Thank you."

"You are welcome. May I know what you're making?" He lifted the lid of the pot to smell the scent the aroma gave off. I playfully slapped his hand away, "No!" I screamed laughing, "It is a surprise, but you'll like it." I smiled at him.

His eyes said he wanted to kiss me. Kissing was the same step we were at and had been the whole time. I never asked if he sought satisfaction from another woman. I didn't blame him if he did. The way his big sea blue eyes stared at me answered my thoughts. For the first time, I kissed him. The kiss was our first kiss. It lasted until the stove had alerted us, the sauce was over boiling.

"Oh gosh," I said with a laugh, avoiding flying sauce.

"Here, I got this." He turned the knob off, keeping his eyes on me.

"Watch what you're doing."

"I'm focused on not letting the one get away from me." His smile took me back to the first time we met.

"The one," I said smiling.

"There's one person for everyone in the whole world."

"If there is one person for everyone in the whole world, how do you know your one is not across the world still waiting for you?"

"Because I've been all around the world and haven't found her until now. See, some people are afraid to leave what they know, mostly because they're afraid what's out there or what they may find. That fear keeps them alone. I'm not afraid of anything, just like our kiss, when you kissed me, showed you aren't afraid anymore. Within time, when you are ready, you will look at me like I look at you and I'll know you love me." Luc kissed me slightly on my cheek. "Now, how can I help you finish? I am starving."

"This is my surprise to you. You can get out of my kitchen. I need to finish."

"Okay, I'll sit on the sofa and watch you finish. Hopefully I can pick up a thing or two to use for work."

His eyes were on me the whole time. Entertaining his eyes was the least of my concerns. Cooking took over my body while I was doing it. No one or thing could cause me distractions. Cooking was my happiness. It was my life. I only wished I had it at my aunt's house. Those days are long gone, now.

"Voilà." I presented the art I had created.

"Wow, it looks too good to eat."

I was an artist through my food. "I'll eat it all if you don't want it," I teased.

"Oh no, I want this. I've been dying for it since I walked through the door."

We laughed together and ate the food I cooked.

"Wow, you're amazing," Luc complimented me.

"Merci beaucoup. Do you really like the meat pie?"

"I love it. I would have preferred a French meal," he confessed.

I debated back, "I like trying new things. I took a gamble."

"And how do you think your gamble did?" He stopped eating to show me his suspenseful face.

"Oh lala la, it paid off," I said. My fork was full of pie crust and meat. My hand swung the fork back and forward, the meat and crust smacked Luc right in the left eye. Luc's face wandered as the food dropped from his eye onto his lap. "Oh, don't laugh!" He looked serious at me.

I couldn't help the smile across my face.

"Bellina, this isn't funny."

"No, you're right. I'm not laughing." I couldn't help myself. I exploded in

laugher. I laughed until several slices of
meat slapped me on the right side of my
mouth.

I heard Luc's laughter in my ear
drums. "Oh you think that's funny?"

I stood with strings of salad in my
hands. "Laugh at this!" I threw the salad
right at him. Luc picked up his plate and
threw the food at me. I threw my glass of
iced tea at him. With that, anything our
hands touched were the things we threw at
each other. It was a night I loved, one I
would always remember. All the food I
cooked ended on Luc or me and the rest of
the house. We fell asleep laughing in each
other's arms. The mess stayed as it was.
Luc's lips kissed my forehead.

"Bellina," he said.

"Yes?" I answered.

"Thank you for dinner." I pulled
myself closer in his arms.

* * *

I entered my third year in school. Every
time I wore my white jacket it felt like
the school made it just for me. The person
who ironed it made sure the lines were
straight and sharp. My jacket smelled
fresh, it felt warm, with the school's

name proudly shown above the upper left
chest.

"Bellina, Bellina!"

My daydream was interrupted by my
instructor handing me the crisp white
apron I was supposed to wear over my white
jacket.

"Thank you." I said a lot of thank
yous that day. My face nearly fell off
from all the smiling I did. The first time
since I had lived in Paris, when I walked
home, greeting the people who passed me on
the street, they greeted me back. The
smiles on the streets made my day
brighter, so bright I saw buildings
smiling at me. My third year was going to
be a good year. I was prepared for all the
stress about to enter my life. I was
excited for it. The years had gone by so
fast.

"*Salut,* Monsieur Berg." I burst in
the shop, "I'm glad you're here. I have so
much to say." I was surprise to see him.
Sharing my news with him made me even more
excited.

"Not so loud." He waved at me.

"Oh, Monsieur Berg, you'll be so
proud of me." I wanted someone to be proud
of me. I didn't want to wait for it. I
wanted to hear it now.

"What did you do?"

"I've made it to my third year."

He finally looked up, then at me.
"Bravo! If I still taught, you're the
exact student I would want in my class."

He smiled slightly at me. I could tell he mentally still wasn't there. He looked the same as my mother when she lost my father. A part of me knew he was ready to go be with her. When was the only question. I had imagined his departure would be soon.

"Bellina, I want you to know you're the best tenant I ever had. I'm glad to have spent this time with you." He held the black and white photo of his young wife tightly in his hand.

I didn't know what to say. His words caught me off guard.

"Would you like to go to a theater with me?" I invited him, hoping an activity would take his mind off the pain that lived in him all of these years.

"You're a nice girl, but I think I'll stay right here. I like to watch the fish swim for a little longer. Would you like to have a seat with me?" The reflection of the fish bowl reflected in his eyes. I sat next to him, admiring the fish he had collected over the years. A postmark letter lay halfway off the bookcase in the corner. I looked closely and noticed letters were scattered everywhere. I turned to him; he was holding a bunch of letters tightly in his hands. My hand embraced his. He held onto the letters as I held onto his hand. "Everything will be fine," I consoled him. We sat in the dark staring at fish with the moonlight shining in.

* * *

Autumn had arrived bringing colors of
orange, red, yellow, and brown. Crisp
leaves fell off trees painting the green
grass that lived underneath them. The
cooler weather sent chills down my spine.
I made it home from school before the
beautiful vibrant colors got lost in the
misty gray skies. The misty gray skies
stayed for a while.

Regardless how the weather was, I
went on a short walk. The walk didn't feel
right, and I wondered if it was because I
hadn't seen Monsieur Berg in a week. When
I had turned the corner to the fish store,
a car was parked outside of it. A man was
leaving the shop. He saw me walking up and
called out to me, "Excuse me,
Mademoiselle, are you Bellina Asma?"

"I am."

"I'm sorry, but Monsieur Heberg
passed away Monday."

Sadness came over me. I had lost a
friend. The man told me not to worry, that
Monsieur Berg had made all of the
arrangements and I could live in the
studio until my studies were over. I
thanked him and went up to my place.
Everything is alright, I thought. Monsieur
Berg was with the girl he loved and I
couldn't be sad about that. He died in his
sleep peacefully the detective told the
news reporter. A neighbor found him
sitting in front of a window. When he

didn't move at the knocks the neighbor
made by hitting on the window, the
neighbor called the police. The funny
thing was that day, the sun shined briefly
during the day. It may have been Monsieur
Berg happy to be back in his lover's arms.

His funeral was a quiet affair, only
a few people showed up. College professors
spoke briefly about Monsieur Berg. None
mentioned his love for his wife or how
they were together at this very second. I
had to say something or they would never
know who he was.

"Pardon me." I stood, addressing the
church from my seat. The wrinkled faces
and black coats turned their attention to
me. "I live above Monsieur Berg's fish
shop. In the studio he rents to students
of the city and, if I may, leave you all
with the memory of the man I knew." I
looked for permission from the priest to
continue. He nodded with approval.

"The first time we met, I thought the
school was crazy to reference me to live
above his shop. I expected the worst to
come out of it and mentally prepared
myself to leave. I didn't have to leave
because I got to know Monsieur Berg.
Monsieur Berg was a romantic man who loved
his wife whom he lost at a young age. He
fought proudly in the war. He taught many
of tomorrow's thinkers. I know he only
lived his days counting down the time
until he would see his beloved again." I
closed my mouth for a second, "Please

don't cry for him because I know he's in love, happy and safe in his wife's arms." I sat down.

"Thank you, mademoiselle. She is right about the man we bury today," the priest continued.

At the end of the service, I left. I walked into the chilly air. The wind blew the color leaves past me. Monsieur Berg's death erupted feelings of my own mother and father's death. I had avoided the scenes in Paris where I once saw my mother smile.

I wanted to rekindle the times we spent together. I had brought a basket of fruits, food, and writing material. I went to where my mother and I spent a whole day at, the Eiffel Tower. An extra scarf kept me warm against the chilly weather. I spent the day on the lawn, writing to my mother. I left out all the bad and the heartache I suffered just to focus on missing them.

I wrote and wrote, pouring all of my experiences as a student in France. I wrote to my father about Luc. I wrote to my mother about being the only woman in my graduating class. When I finished the night had come. My food was left untouched and scattered letters were all around me. I bundled the letters, vowing never to forget the good times we shared together. I knew I couldn't turn back the time, but at the moment I felt strong that my parents were right by my side.

Luc came by a day after the service. "I was looking for you yesterday." Luc sat on the sofa with open arms for me.

"You missed the service."

"I know, I do not know," he answered unsurely.

"You do not know what?" I asked.

"Monsieur Berg and I never were fond of each other. I did not want to be the odd ball in the crowd," Luc said.

"Ah, don't give yourself that much credit. You're probably the least odd ball in that church," I assured him.

"Uh." He looked at me, unsure, "Like I said before. I came here to talk to you about something else."

"What would you like to talk about?"

"Hmmm, how was your day?" he asked me. I looked hopelessly at him. "Come on," he said, grabbing my hand.

"Let's go. How was your day, Luc Christian?" I asked him.

"It's been good, my love." He grabbed my hand, twirled me around, "It's getting better by the minute."

"I agreed," I squealed. Our days became filled with magic. We danced in the streets on clear and rainy days.

"I got the manager-in-training position at work."

"Congratulations!"

"Does this mean you won't be able to see me as much?"

"A little I want to advance in my career. That way, one day, I could open a restaurant and put you as my head chef."

"Oh, that's if I decide to work for you," I teased.

"I'll give you a great health package, competitive pay, and recognition beyond your wildest dreams. Working for me would be Heaven on earth."

"Heaven on earth? Hun, I'll settle for peace on earth."

"Easy to please, you seem to be."

"At times I can be, but today I'll like to relax," I said.

"Relax like I'm living on a cloud," I told him.

Luc came behind me, scooping me in his arms. "If you want to relax like you're in a cloud, I'll carry you so you can feel like you're floating home." He carried me home like he was holding me as if he was protecting an angel that hadn't learned to fly. I was the angel. People moved out of our way. We were the lovely couple in the city of love.

"Your studio above awaits you, my love." Luc put me down in front of the fish shop.

Monsieur Berg gave me a copy of the key to the door. The realtor had the real key and only showed the fish shop. She had to wait until I moved to show the studio. The cleaning crew came that morning to take the fish and clean.

"They did a good job in that short time," Luc said. They did. By the time we came back, the place had no sign of a fish shop or Monsieur Berg. "Don't think about his death and you'll be fine."

"I know, it feels …" I tried to get the words out. "The feeling is different. I'll come home to my studio. No fish to feed, no one to tell how my day had been." We walked up to my studio.

"I can move in with you if you like?" He hugged me.

"Ah, I'm not ready for everyday company."

"I wouldn't be company."

"I know. I'm not ready for that," I told him.

"That's fine. Slow is the pace we're moving."

"Yes, slow," I said laughing.

"I better get going. I'll see you tomorrow if I can get away from work." Luc kissed me goodnight. I fell asleep on the sofa. The day exhausted me. The sunshine woke me before my alarm could. The morning was beautiful.

My morning became a challenge. The bath water never ran hot, no matter how many times I tried to fix it. I stopped, drained, and restarted it. I had no choice but to take a cold bath. Before I could jump out, I had my towel open, ready to wrap around me. My coffee pot quit working, along with the flat iron. Worse, I was late leaving for class.

My mood for the day was ruined. I left cold and unmotivated. The beautiful morning had treated me well. Summer had arrived. Instead of taking a break from school, I decided to take the summer course the school offered. Most of the students who wanted to be head chef at the school's restaurant were taking the summer courses. They signed up for other resources outside the school; I didn't.

I walked the circle of the center square. I wanted to get lost for the day. It was something I hoped for. I thought back on my time living in Paris. I hadn't been lost in the city for a while. I walked to the garden to see the different colors of the flowers. The flowers smelled so fresh. I was lying on the ground in the middle of the reds, pinks, oranges, yellows, purples, and whites. I picked one and smelled it.

I shrunk ten sizes and climbed into the petals of the flowers. Inside became the safest place for me to dream my wildest dreams. I dreamt I was a fairy lying on a lone red rose petal, floating on a pond. The water was crystal clear and felt cool between my fingers. Lily petals swam around me. I heard applause from behind.

"I don't know too many women who sleep with smiles on their faces." The unfamiliar voice had disturbed my daydreams. "Nor do I know beautiful women who lie on the ground."

I opened my eyes to the familiar face.

"I'm sorry to disturb you. It's not every day I come across a sleeping beauty," he said. "Here, let me help you up."

I tried to stand, but only stumbled back down right into my admirer's arms. He looked into my eyes as if he knew me.

"May I draw you?"

"What?" I said. I wasn't attractive to him. He had short curly black hair, brown eyes, thin lips, and average built. Blocking the sunlight with my hand, I realized he was the lone painter I had seen several times before. "It's you!" I said in disbelief. He smiled down at me.

"Have we met before?" he asked as he searched my face for answers.

"No, I saw you painting," I answered shyly.

"Oh yes, I try not to make myself known to people," he shyly said.

"You're not good at it." We stood in the middle of the garden. "What made you come over here?" I asked as we started to walk.

"I needed a change of scenery. Why were you sleeping in the middle of flowers? You don't have a bed at home?" He smiled at his own joke.

"Very funny," I answered. He then grabbed my arm as he stepped in front of me. He held out his hands in a photo frame way in front of my face. "That's how I want to draw you, in a garden of roses."

"What color roses?"

"Colors the roses are behind you." He rubbed my cheek with his back hand. "It seems I got lucky today. I found a beautiful new muse."

Like that, I was his muse. I love that I was going to be the center of attention.

"Come by next week. My studio is the last one on the left city corner, 147 East. Just come in. Be there by one Friday."

I waved, not sure what I had gotten myself into. The only thing I knew was I had met the lone painter whom I had thought about often. He had come to me. I couldn't wait for Friday to come.

* * *

"Welcome, everyone. I expect great dishes within these four weeks from everyone because I'm in a kitchen of top achievers." Mr. Borax's eyed the class with a stern face. He was tall and thin. He looked more like a science professor than a culinary genius.

The class was going to be tough competition. I knew the next four weeks would make or break dreams for the following year. The nine people surrounding me wanted to be head chef. All were great cooks. There wasn't one in the room who couldn't be the head chef.

"You all should be able to cook a course meal. Don't worry, it's not what you're about to do. I want each of you to create a dish that expresses you. Tell me where you're from. What your mum used to cook for you. Don't treat my kitchen like a mad house. Keep your stations clean. I give you forty minutes; you may begin."

For the first five minutes, the pots and pans slammed together making music I had never heard recorded. The fire sizzled on the gas stove. Dishes got started; I was behind. I thought of the dish that would express me. I create many dishes, but none I would put my existence on. What would I want my mum to make me, pounded in my head. Just a soup; all I wanted was soup that felt warm going down and made me want to be home. I grilled the chicken while the broth sat while others sample theirs. I kept cooking and cutting my meat. I added chopped carrots, greens, and tofu into the broth. I allowed all the ingredients to cook before I added the chicken.

I fixed a bowl of the soup putting it on a plate. I broke off a small piece French of bread I pulled from the oven and dipped it into the bowl of soup. I beat the time by three seconds.

"Time is up." He went to us each, tasting while we explained our dishes. "Very interesting,"

He examined my chicken soup. "Plain and simple." He glanced up at me, then dunked the French bread in the soup. Mr. Borax shoved the bread with the soup dripping from it, into his mouth.

Several drops made it back into the bowl, spiraling in circles. He walked past me, turning around. "Bravo!" He winked at me, continuing to the next station. The smile on my face said it all. It was that he loved it. It was a simple dish of chicken soup. I put in a bowl that expressed me. I dunked the other slice of French bread in the bowl of soup and stuffed the whole slice into my mouth. I caught several eyes staring my way. I stared back. I wasn't tempted by the others; I was a chef. I made no apologies.

"I'm impressed with all of you. Simple dishes to combinations I haven't heard before. All were good. Today was the easy part. I got to know where all of you come from through what food you grew up on, the food your mum cooked for you. By the end of these four weeks I'll know you. My recommendations for head chef for your four year class will be given to the committee at that time as well. Those not affiliated with the institution will gain extra experience and knowledge through this class. If you're attending another school, make sure you check if your credits are transferable. You'll receive your credits at the end," Mr. Borax explained. Not all nine attending the class were students of the school, I was relieved to know.

The summer course was three hours, Monday through Friday, in the morning. It left the whole afternoon and evening for me to enjoy my summer.

"I'm delighted to say, I look forward to seeing you all, tomorrow." He dismissed us. Of all my instructors, I took a liking to Mr. Borax. He took to the art of food unlike the others. I took the long way through the city to the cafe.

* * *

"Hello, is Luc here?" I took a seat at one of the tables.

"Ah Bellina, I'll get him for you," said the cafe owner, Jean.

"Thank you. I'll be right here."

Luc was tending to customers outside. He didn't notice me. The summers were just as bad as the winter. Customers lined up for the ice coffees and sandwiches the cafe was famous for, time escape without attention to. I had been sitting at the table for over two hours.

"Jean, if you'll like for me to move," I volunteered.

"Oh no, no, no, you can stay here as
long as you like," he insisted as if I was
family.

"Did you tell Luc I was here?"

"Yes, he said he'll be right over.
He's just a little busy." With that Jean
was gone to deal with the broken cups in
the kitchen. I stayed put for another
hour, looking at the many sights of Luc.
Finally I got up to leave.

"Bellina, wait."

I was halfway out the door when Luc
stopped me. "I'm so, so, so sorry."

"It's alright. I needed to sit for a
while," I lied.

"Did you eat anything?" Luc looked
tired, "Come back in. I haven't had
anything to eat all day."

"Okay, I'll stay a little longer."

"Great. Sorry I've been so busy; this
may be the only time I'll have to spend
with you today."

"I know you're a manager trainee now,
more responsibilities."

"Yes, you know if you allowed me to
move in with you, I could come home
overnight to you."

I laughed at his persistence. "We're
not living together," I assured him.

"I'm sorry to hear that." He made a
dopey face.

"Aww, aww, you'll be alright."

"Hun, I think my heart is breaking."
He acted out as if his heart broke in
half. I got out of my seat to close his

hands into a shaped heart. He quickly swung his hands around my head and kissed me. "Maybe I'll ask tomorrow."

"You can, I'll not change my mind."

"You never know. A lot can happen in twenty-four hours."

I sat back down. Luc signaled to Jean.

"I know you don't expect me to wait on you. You know your way around the kitchen. Get in there and fix your own meal," Jean yelled at Luc.

"See? I can't even take a break for myself. What would you like, my love?" We sat holding hands.

"I want a turkey sandwich," I said.

"To drink, my love," Luc said with a smiled, that I loved to look at.

"I'll have a berry tea, please."

"I love you very much. I want you to know that." He looked at me seriously. I said nothing, smiling back. "I'm going to make your sandwich before I give you a chance to break my heart again." He blew a kiss at me. I pretended to catch it. Though his heart broke, I managed to keep a smile on his face. This cafe was the place we first met, one of my favorite places in the city. The plates, the cling, crashing, the coffee brewing, the cabinets opening and closing, the phone ringing, the people talking, kissing each other, smiling saying their *bonjours, au revoirs*; mostly I loved how people a painted picture of walking on the streets with their lovers, children, friends and that every day the picture changed.

"Here you go." Luc came back with my sandwich in hand.

"Luc, I need you now," Jean said.

"As you heard, I must go. Eat, drink, and be merry. I'll stop by tonight if it's not too late."

Before I could say anything, Luc left. I did as I was told, then left. I found my way back to my studio. I tipped around my studio. My day was over. I looked forward to Luc's coming over more than I thought.

Downstairs was too quiet since Monsieur Berg's death. I wanted some company. Night fell; Luc never showed. I went to bed, but found it hard to stay asleep through the night. I couldn't get my true feelings of Luc out of my head. The truth was, I was scared to love him and thought it would be best if he knew.

Chapter 12

We stood at our tables in our white
jackets and aprons ready for whatever dish
Mr. Borax was about to throw our way, like
the cowboy ready to draw his gun during a
dual. We were ready to pull our sharpest
knives and freshest ingredients into a
mixture of food in our silver pans. We
were ready. Bring it on, is what our
jackets said.

"Today pick a country to make a dish
from. You will have forty minutes to
complete your dish. You may begin," he
instructed. This challenge was meant for
me. Of all the countries Ms. Hickens and I
visited, today's class was a piece of
cake. I thought to not be simple and wild
Mr. Borax with spice and tangy. I wanted
his eyes to pop out from his head from the
firing peppers I was about to use.

"Time," Mr. Borax began walking
around. The first dish left his face
plain. "Your dish could be better if the
shrimp were sauté a little more." Then he
spoke to the whole class, "Forty minutes
isn't a short time to make one dish. Don't
be afraid of the time. Now what do you
have for me." He put the fork in his
mouth. His face crunched. As fast as the
fork full of food went in his mouth, it
came back out. "This is trash.

Disgusting," he yelled, throwing the plate into the trash. "What are you doing in my class, if you don't know how to cook."

The boy started to say something. Mr. Borax cut him off. "You make another dish like this, don't come back!" he said, moving on to the next station. "I hope you have something better!"

"I do," said the boy.

There were some so-so dishes, none made his face excited, or made him want to leave Paris without a passport and weekend clothes. He hadn't explored any cultures until he came to my station. My dish was so good. I knew he was about to go house hunting in Mexico. I already booked his trip.

"Bravo!" I knew his eyes were ready to go.

"Here's your plane ticket!" I said.

He looked at me. I still hadn't realized, my thoughts were said out loud.

"You think that's funny."

"No, it's not." I tried to recover fast, but my recovery wasn't the recovery that would get me out of the sick bed. "No sir, that's not what I meant."

"Please explain what it's you meant." He wasn't smiling.

"I mean you wanted to explore. You wanted to leave Paris and that's what I allowed you to do." I searched the floor for the biggest shoe to get ready to stuff down my throat. He pointed his finger at me. "Don't allow me to hear you smart off again."

I shook my head. "I won't." He moved on, eyeing me. I looked at the clock, wishing twelve o'clock came soon. Once he was finished tasting our dishes, he stood in front of us.

"It's true. I did want to explore different countries today. Only three of you took me on that journey. Tomorrow, I expect greatness from all of you. If you're not prepared to give me that, don't waste my time coming."

We left with bitter tastes in our mouth. I knew I was one of the three, with my great Mexican dish. I knew to keep my mouth closed next time.

* * *

Friday came around without the sights of Luc. I stayed busy getting myself together to become the lone painter's muse. I heard painters like their canvas blank. I put on a pair of jeans and white shirt. I was as plain as plain could be.

I walked to the corner with the piece of paper with the address in my hand. I headed to it. I arrived at somewhat of a wooden shack on the corner. It looked dark and gloomy, as if it had been waiting on a visitor for a long time.

The doors squeaked as it opened to a wooden staircase. A block of sunshine led the way to the top. I ignored the darkness of the empty downstairs. I ran upstairs, running before the wooden stairs broke beneath me.

"Well, I see you found your way here," the lone painter said.

"Yes, lone painter, I made it." I laughed. "I'm sorry. I don't know your name. I've been calling you lone painter all this time," I said, confused. He laughed back.

"It's alright. My name is Gabriel, and you are?" He searched my eyes for an answer, like he could guess before I told him.

"Bellina." Upstairs was a relief compared to the downstairs. The sun shined in the huge studio. Canvases were everywhere surrounding Gabriel's bed. Paint decorated the floor, the canvas, and parts of the wall, beautiful paintings of landscapes covered with green grass, a dirt road and blue sky. There were paintings of women posed as goddesses. I thought how lovely they looked and how I could look just as lovely.

Gabriel was mysterious; he was the complete opposite of Luc. He took off his shirt. He bore his muscles and chest. "I work better shirtless."

"It had made me uncomfortable, but as long as your pants stayed on, I was okay to handle it."

"What would you like me to do?" I
shyly asked. I was ready to become a muse.

"Anything you like."

I hadn't moved from the spot I was
standing at. "Oh."

"You can start by getting
comfortable. You look like you're about to
dash back down the stairs and out the
door."

"I'm not," I answered back in the
same position. "I've never done this
before. I'm a bit nervous."

"Done what?"

"Be someone's inspiration." I perked
up. He started to set up his easel.

"I thought you were going to paint me
in the garden?" I asked.

"Yes, I do a testing here first, then
I move to my destination. I plan to paint
you in the garden surrounded by exotic
flowers."

"Exotic!"

"You're exotic to me." He sat in
front of his easel.

"I am not exotic." There was nothing
exotic about me.

"Exotic is great; a flower in a bed
of roses. That's a beautiful thing."

"Trust me, you are," he debated back
at me.

"I don't want to be like every other
girl you painted. I want something
different. I want to feel different." I
clearly stated my purpose for becoming his
muse. I wanted to feel different as if I

was the only one. "Why are you staring at me that way?"

"This painting will bring the light back to your eyes. I'll make sure of it," he said.

I had paused, thinking of the best response. There was none; nothing came to mind to say.

"Don't worry," he said. "You're the main focus for this painting, and everyone will see the light in your eyes."

I had been the focus in my parents, Aunt Michelle, Ms. Hickens, and Luc's eyes, but this was different. There were no distractions, no work, no drinking, no school, no love. Gabriel only wanted me. He craved my attention and no other. Just like a star in the sky, he wanted to bring out the light in me. I was ready to let that happen.

The day I went to class, Mr. Borax had us watch a video of famous chefs of Paris. It was nice not to cook. He taught us the history in the eyes of former chefs. A lot of cooking classrooms wouldn't think to offer that. If we wanted something to snack on, we had to make it ourselves. I just watched the film, getting full on their knowledge.

When I arrived home, the shop's door was open. I made sure no one was around before I went in. Nothing had been touched; I thought the realtor had forgotten to close the door. Out of nowhere I heard a door closing and noticed

my studio door slightly opened. I ran up
the stairs to investigate who was in my
studio.

"What are you doing here?" I
screamed. I slammed the door open. "I
thought you were a stranger!"

"Calm down, I came here looking for
you. I haven't seen you in a couple of
weeks, so I thought to bring you lunch.
The realtor let me in." Luc got up from my
bed. A bunch of my letters fell to the
floor.

"What are you doing in my dresser?
All my letters; those were private." I
rushed to pick them up and find the
correct order they were in.

"I'm sorry. I did not know who they
were from. Here, sit on the bed." Luc sat
me on the bed. Tears had already made
their way down my face.

"Luc, these are private letters." My
hands shook as I held the letters that
were written about me.

"You can't keep this secret hidden.
You'll never have closure. Don't do that
to yourself. You know, you deserve to love
and live. These letters are keeping you
back from living and loving me." I could
only look at him. My throat was caught
with lumps of saliva and my chest burned
with heartache.

"I'm sorry, I'm really am. After all
of these years together, why couldn't you
talk to me about this?"

"Are you rationalizing why you did this? I don't have to talk to you about this. This is mine!" I shouted.

"Right, it's your hurt and pain, and I'm just on for the ride as you try to get it together," he shouted back.

I turned my back to him. "That's not true. I've never thought of you in that way," I softly said to him.

"Then what is it?"

"I always thought you didn't want to hear about my problems."

"That's a lie," he interrupted me.

"Why couldn't you wait for me to tell you when I was ready?"

"When did you plan on doing so?" he demanded. I remained silent. "Bellina, I can't keep being the only one trying in this relationship. By now we should have developed something so strong; we should be on a road to talking about having a family."

I looked at him. "A family? Luc, I'm here to start a career, not to start a family," I coldly said.

The anger in his eyes spoke for him. "You can have both." His anger transferred to hope. "But you don't want that." As fast as his hope was high it went back down. Moments of silence passed before I could open my mouth. It was too late.

"When you're ready to want something more, you know where to find me." Luc turned to leave. He stopped at the door and sighed. He was waiting on me to stop

him. After realizing I wasn't, he closed
the door behind him, leaving me standing
in scattered letters.

I kept my distance from the café. I
did care and missed him. I just wanted to
make my career happen.

* * *

Friday finally arrived; I was thrilled I
was going to have my portrait painted. I
had been looking forward to it all week. I
went straight to his studio.

"One hazelnut flavor cup of coffee
for the beauty sitting alone." Gabriel
greeted me with a cup of coffee. "Be
careful, it's hot."

I sipped the coffee. "Hmmm, this is
really good."

He drank his walking toward the
window.

"I'm ready to get started," I told
him.

I heard the gulp of coffee go down
his throat. "It's going to rain. Would you
like to sleep here tonight?" he asked.
Outside looked stormy. The clouds were
gray; people traveled wearing their
raincoats with umbrellas tucked underneath
their arms.

"No, I have a place to go home to," I
bluntly said to him.

"I thought I should offer," he said.

"Are you ready to start the painting?" I couldn't wait any longer.

"From the moment I saw you I was ready to paint you," he flattered me. I laughed at his silly line. "Are you comfortable with nudity?" His question stopped my laugher.

"No, I don't wish to be naked," I replied to him.

"Okay, you're my muse. Tell me what makes you feel beautiful and I'll interpret that into the painting." The question was simple, but it stopped me like a bullet through the heart. Luc made me feel beautiful. The way his blue eyes looked at me made me feel beautiful, and at the moment I missed him dearly and wanted him to come back badly. The painting was supposed to be about me; instead, it made me feel as if I had a heartless soul.

"Bellina," Gabriel called out to me. "Hello?"

Too upset to explain I ran out crying into the storm in the night. I leaned on the corner of a building for support, crying my heart out. My feelings I had tarnished toward Luc had resurfaced. I crossed my arms, hugging myself in them. I thought about how awful I treated him, allowing him to leave my heart when he cared about me so much. I cried at how upset I was for pushing him away. The rain poured down on me. A voice came to me like an angel giving me his wing, "Come with me!" He covered me and picked me off the ground. "It'll be alright. Trust me, I'll take you inside." I was out of the rain and safe in his arms. He carried me up the stairs back into the place I left.

"Is your foot alright?" he asked once we were inside.

"Ouch!" I yelled. The touch sent waves of pain throughout my body. "That really hurts."

"I saw you trip on the broken step when you rushed out of here. You're going to have to get out of those wet clothes before you catch pneumonia. Then I want you to get off your foot," he said. I was shaking all over. "It's okay," He told me. He started a fire as I went to change in the bathroom. "Don't worry, the fire heats the room fast. In no time your chill will go away. There are plenty of towels on the rack. In the basket is a long shirt for you to wear," he called to me. I tried not to put pressure on my foot. The more I tried, the more I wanted to.

"Ouch!" I screamed. "I think I broke it." I choked up, standing in the doorway of the bathroom.

"No, you didn't. Here let me help you." He left a pot of boiling water and rushed over to help lift my foot. I ended up on the bed dressed only in a shirt, "Don't move." He went back over to turn the knob off, pouring the boiling water into a cup and adding honey and green leaves. "Drink this, it's tea. My mom used to make it for me. She called it a healing tea that takes all your pain away."

I pulled myself up slightly to sip on the tea. He handed me the tea and went to the edge of the bed.

"Ouch!" I cried, when he touched my sore foot.

"So this is the spot. Breathe, then sip on the tea." I did as instructed; ignoring the pain I felt as he lifted my foot and put it on his leg. He slowly massaged my whole foot, releasing the ache I felt. "Is that better?"

"Yes." He massaged my foot until I finished my tea.

"I'll take the cup." I handed it to him. "Rest now. Everything will be fine in the morning." He crawled next to me. "I'll sing to you, but I'm afraid I'm not a good singer."

"That's okay." He made me smile. I didn't sleep throughout the night. That voice that picked me up and took care of me kept me smiling at him. We didn't touch; only the fire kept us warm as we smiled the whole night.

"I'm glad I found you."

"Me, too," I said.

"Goodnight," the voice said. My angel's voice, my angel Gabriel, I thought. We slept past the morning and well into the evening.

* * *

"Good morning," I said, rolling
around to shake the sleep away.
"Good evening," Gabriel said.
"Is it still the night?"
"It's tomorrow night."
"Ohh, we slept the whole day." I sat
up. Gabriel stood there dressed.
"Are you planning to finish the
painting anytime soon?" I asked.
"All good things come in good time. I
mustn't rush my work." He looked at me.
"I'm a professional. We'll get started
today."
I carefully stood, avoiding
submitting my foot to anymore pain.
"How does your foot feel?"
"It feels much better." I pressed on
the foot that I had twisted, "It really
does feel better," I surprisingly said.
"The healing tea works. Thank you,
mom." He looked up and winked at the
ceiling. I had walked around in a line
from the bed to the window. I wished the
fire hadn't quit burning, realizing the
warmth had made me feel beautiful. The
moment held its silence as I heard the
penciling of Gabriel's art begin.
I didn't bother to look behind me; I
decided to let the professional create his
masterpiece. I traveled my thoughts to the
garden, a garden at the end of a
waterfall. That was the place I was at. My
hotel wasn't book for my stay. There

wasn't need for sleep for where I was
sleeping was not allowed. I lie on the
soft grass to restore the energy taken
away from me.

The fireflies shine their light above
me, telling me I was completely charge.
The butterflies take their place, waving
their colors, inviting me to come and
dance with them. The dance attracts the
doves, who lend me their feathers to make
a beautiful garment for dinner with the
swans. I ate their food and drank from
their beaks as the dolphin appears and
says, "Come swim with me."

"Here I come, dolphin!" I giggled
when the dolphin gave me his fin for me to
hold on to, for my swim. He drove me to
the fall where the water showered me.
Light shined brightly as the water cleanse
my skin. At the end of my travel the
flowers bloom once more, for my joyous
return. How beautiful the place came to
be. Because it's in my dreams; how
beautiful it will stay.

"I love watching you think," Gabriel
said. "It makes me want to paint you
more."

"You want to paint me more?"

"If I could, I would paint you all
the time." I saw him stroke the brush on
his canvas. The stroke was exactly how I
imagined an artist would curve his hand to
outline his figure. "My Bella, my," he
whispered, eyeing me, then his work. I
stood in front of the window. The position

I was standing wasn't attractive or easy
on the eyes. I learned the unattractive
are the people artists love the most. The
afternoons I had for free time was now
time with Gabriel.

* * *

The morning I woke in my own bed with my
sleep wearing off. It felt so good to lie
between my blankets with my pillow in my
arms. Today I had to make a sweet dessert.
Everyone would be making something for the
whole class. I needed to be different to
keep standing out. I couldn't cook with
anymore peppers. I didn't want Mr. Borax
thinking that was all I knew.
      I wanted colors to paint the plate
with. Berries were colorful. Yes, I could
make a spice cake, topped with ripe
berries, with a scoop of vanilla bean ice
cream, topped with a circle of caramel
sauce and a caramel brittle. My stomach
rumbled at the thought of the cake,
beautiful; what a wonderful summer
dessert. I jumped out of bed. My tub water
ran the way I liked the temperature. I
slid down into the tub. Bubbles filled the
tub floating around me. In each bubble I
saw a rainbow. Ms. Hickens introduced me
to sea salt. I poured some into my tub. I
soaked for an hour.

When I thought I was clean I got out, drying and putting my clothes on. I brushed my hair, admiring my face in the mirror. The painting had given me a confidence I hadn't had before. I felt like I could take on the world. I took the longer route to class. I figured I could get inspiration from something on the way. I was right; the vendors were up early preparing food for their customers. I inhaled the scent of the spices. I got inspired by the colors people wore. I lined up in class with a good feeling in me. Today was the day I had to be prompt. This outlined the future I wanted to achieve at this school.

"Good morning. Today I'll be expecting each of you to present a three course meal," Mr. Borax said. I knew I was going to make the spice cake, an apple sage butternut squash soup for an appetizer, but I stood stunned about the main course. All this time and I never thought about making a main dish. I stood there dumbfounded. I could make a quail, I quickly thought. Yes, a quail stuffed with something, but what?

For the first time I stumbled. I did want to create mouthwatering dishes that exploded the taste buds with excitement. I thought about making a seafood stuffed filet mignon. It wouldn't go together with my soup and I didn't think anyone would like me stuffing a filet. Mr. Borax wasn't the only one tasting our courses; he had

invited two instructors to taste the food
we created. All of the meals were on the
table. We were having a feast.

"In the culinary world, wine tasting
is paired with your dishes. I brought
fifteen bottles for you all to choose
from. The wine tasting is optional, but
preferred. If you would like to make a
special drink, you may do so," Mr. Borax
offered, "You may begin."

I worked fiercely with the time
being. I tried not to think about the big
picture in the end. My mind focused on
creating an amazing three course meal. I
still had to pair a wine to my course. I
would have paired a flavor tea with the
food, but that wasn't going to get me to
the top.

To pair my food, I had to taste the
wine. No time to second guess my decision
to taste the wine or not; I did it without
thinking of my promise to myself to never
drink alcohol. It's okay, I said, I'm not
drinking to get drunk; it's just a
tasting, I assured myself. I worked
through the hot kitchen preparing my
meals. The heat from all of the stoves
made me want to take my jacket off. I
thought I was in a sauna.

The smell from the kitchen was beyond
outstanding. It reminded me I was
completing against the top of my class to
get the position as head chef at our
restaurant. The scent around me made me
concentrate more on what I making. The

butter in my pan sizzled. The water
boiling in my pot steamed. I felt my
confidence turn on full-blown. I got in a
rhythm as I cooked. From that point on no
one else cooked in the kitchen, only me.
My plating was stunning, I thought. The
food filled the plate with color like I
had imagined in my head. "Time is almost
up. Finish plating, then you'll present
your courses to us," Mr. Borax said. I
finished my courses right then along with
the other students.

"Please present your courses," he
said. We sat at the empty seat with the
fixed plate in front of me. The three
instructors had begun eating the
appetizers. They carried smiles as they
tasted what looked like a feast.

"What I have for you is an apple and
sage butternut squash soup, a prosciutto
wrapped quail, stuffed with bacon, figs
and cheese. For dessert, I made a
chocolate cerise en vin rouge. I was
introduced to cooking by my surrogate
mother. Since then I have loved cooking,"
I explained.

"Why did you stuff the quail with
fig, bacon, and cheese?" one of the
instructors asked.

"I just thought of it." I threw my
hands up as to surrender to the food.

"You just mixed them together and
stuffed it into the quail?" he asked.

"Yes, I wanted to try something new,"
I said. I was pleased with my

presentation. I knew the greatest chefs learned from their mothers. To me, Ms. Hickens was my other mother, also my best friend. She would have loved to be here.

She would have loved to eat this feast. Ms. Hickens wasn't the only one on my mind; so were my parents. I knew they were smiling proudly upon me. I had a satisfied feeling knowing Mr. Borax's reviews were next. We were all waiting for him to come with our results.

"Let us clear our table and come back to it." Once we were back at the table, Mr. Borax started our review. "Now here are your reviews. For the most part, I was astonished by all of your meals. I was hoping to arrive at class and eat this kind of food.

Believe it or not, you'll experience that many times just like you would get a group of vegetarians. Yes, they're out, and their number is rising. I'm telling you this because I want you to be prepared for all obstacles. You should be able to cook and provide a great experience for any group that comes into your restaurant. I'll be revealing who I think should be considered to run the restaurant to our school's president. He'll decide then."

I tried not to show how irritated I was to have to wait to know who Mr. Borax recommended to run the restaurant. At this level of the game our table should be filled with food out of the standard of thinking. For the most part Mr. Borax didn't have to tell that to anyone anymore. We all had proven ourselves. "This is our last week. I want to concentrate on your plating. We'll be designing your food to look like art on your plate. I'll teach you how to design without over-designing. You're now excused."

I went over to Mr. Borax, "Mr. Borax, can you at least tell me how my food tasted?" I bluntly asked him. I just had to know; the suspense was killing me. He looked at me with hesitation, but I was persistent. "Please," I begged. He sat on the corner of his desk.

"I wanted more than a soup from you," he said. "We all loved the quail and were impressed with the skills it took for you to make it. Bellina, this is a profession you're going to do very well in."

"Thank you," I told him wishing he'd just told me if he was going to recommend me or not.

I took off my jacket folding it not to get it dirty and I left heading home to my studio to drop off my utensils and change to go back to Gabriel. He passed the penciling detail and wanted to start painting today. I could allow Gabriel to paint me all day, forever. I thought of myself more than being a muse. The painting Gabriel was creating. I could truly call mine. I opened the old door and ran up the stairs.

"I'm here!" I alerted Gabriel.

"Me, too. I've been here all day."

"Waiting on me?" I hoped.

"*Oui*, waiting to see my inspiration," he said, "I've never seen a smile so big," he added. "I hope to be the reason behind it."

"I think I made it," I said as a hyper feeling took over my body.

"Really? Well, congratulations, let's get started, beautiful. Pretend like I'm not here. You're here by yourself. I want you to embark in your thoughts and live them out." And that's what I did, only I was not pretending; I truly thought I was the only one in the room. I didn't move around for a while. I didn't come to stand. I went to uncover the mirror. I centered it and just stared into it. I visualized a woman who replicated me, staring back. She stood with her shoulders up high. She was healthy and happy. I was lucky to be her. I forgot about Gabriel painting me. I walked to the window, I'm about to have all of my wishes come true, I told myself. I lifted the window. "Heyyyy," I called out, waving. I thought I saw him.

Chapter 13

"Dramatic is what your plate should say." Mr. Borax made us a plate of food, to begin our last lesson with plating. "I end with plating because I want all of you to remember cooking is an art. Your customers need to remember your work, not just the taste. I want you to come back to me, telling me your customers praise your work. Love, love, love is what they should say."

He brought the plate over so we could examine it. "Start studying designs of art, shapes, and colors. This is what separates the best from the great. Why? Because dishes need to look like they are an award winning art design. Now, that doesn't mean every dish has to be elegantly plated. But appearances do apply in food. Even if you own some hamburger cafe, always dress your plate. Now, I want you to cook breakfast. Remember, dress your plate."

We began cooking to dress our plate. I made an egg soufflé with a green bean and bacon salad, and I mixed some fresh berries to add to a smoothie. The finishing touches were orange slices in the salad. I was proud of my dish; it told who I was as a chef. Mr. Borax came by and looked at our dishes. He didn't taste

anyone's. He nodded if he liked the plate.
He ignored the ones he didn't.

"If I didn't nod at you, then go home
and play around with designs and colors.
Now you may leave."

* * *

I met with Gabriel after my class. My
attention randomly distracted to men
walking by who reminded me of Luc. I
thought I saw him several times.

"Are you ready for me?" I yelled to
him.

"Always. We are still pretending
today."

I picked up where we left off. This
time I stared back at the girl in the
mirror.

"What are you thinking?" Gabriel
asked.

"There's a girl who picked up her
head for the first time in a long time."

"And who is this girl?"

I wasn't ready to answer his
question, "She needs more time."

"More time for what?"

"To speak."

"Tell her she can have all the time
in the world," Gabriel said.

"She doesn't need all the time in the
world; just today."

"I'll give her today then."

"Thank you."

He left me alone. I saw the shape of my figure. The little curve my hips made me feel somewhat of a woman. I turned sideways to look at my side. I stood straight, picking my head up.

"You look vibrant with life."

"I feel that way."

"Keep thinking about whatever is making you feel you are."

There hadn't been a thought in my mind. I felt good about myself, nothing else.

I made it my mission to keep my back straight and my head high.

I watched him paint me. "Have you ever wondered what life would be like if you were another person?" he asked.

"Not another person; I've always pictured myself as a fairy. A fairy, that flies around without a care in the world. They have no problems."

"Nah, everything, everyone has problems; it's just different from the others."

I smiled. "Right. Spreading magic dust around the world is a problem I wouldn't mind having."

"I suppose that would be a nice gig." He smiled.

"Have you dreamed of being someone else?"

He didn't answer; he just kept painting. He didn't need to answer. I saw

his eyes. For the most part he was content
with his life.

"When you're not painting, where do
you go? What do you do?"

He laughed. "I only leave to get
inspiration or to eat."

"You have some life."

"It fulfills me. Not everyone can
live the way that I do."

"I guess that's all that matters."

"You mean nothing if you're not doing
what you love. I mean waking up every
morning to execute what you dreamt of last
night. You're blessed because you are able
to cook. Cooking is what you love. You
wake up to do what you love."

"I guess I am blessed. Ms. Hickens
taught me everything I know. The school
will give me the seal paper I need to show
my knowledge for it."

"She was your teacher?"

"More like a mother to me. You'll
love her and she would love you. She
changes people's lives. She sure did
mine."

"You speak highly of her. I like
that. I like you. Honest people are hard
to find."

"I like you, too." He looked so sad.
I wish I had a way for Ms. Hickens to meet
him. His life would change, "I'm glad you
like me."

"I'm glad we introduced ourselves,"
he said

"Gabriel?"

"Yes?"

"I thought of you as my angel, the night you carried me out of the rain."

"I don't feel like an angel."

"Trust me, you're mine."

He laughed. "I'm qualified to be an angel?"

"You received your winds that night, I believe." I got up and he pulled me back down.

"I think of you more as mine," he said. "Tomorrow we'll meet at the garden." He finished quickly. I couldn't wait to meet him at the garden; finally my portrait would be completed. The excitement burst inside me.

I couldn't wait to see my portrait. We got started right away in the garden. The weather was prefect; the roses were still in full bloom. Being a muse in the garden wasn't how I portrayed it to be. After hours of standing still, I grew restless.

"Please stop moving. You're coming between me and perfection."

"Gabriel, I've been standing here all day." I walked to Gabriel.

"Stop right there! Don't come any closer," he warned me. "I'm not finished with my painting. I cannot afford to lose my steady rhythm."

"Oh, did you find a buyer?"

"No, but I have an idea of where will be my first place of choice."

"Where?"

"Be quiet so I can finish and we'll talk about it."

Gabriel's focus intensified. He stressed out over everything. I had had about enough of his rude direction. More and more, being with Gabriel as he painted me was becoming a nightmare.

"Gabriel, I'm taking a break. You can come with me or stay here." I got up, leading the way.

"Wait, here I come," Gabriel shouted at me. We left the paint and went out to enjoy the streets.

"Where would you like to go first?" I asked.

"I know the place I think you'll love."

"Where is that?" I asked

"The bells of the cathedral. I like to go into the tower and listen to the bells play."

"What do they normally play?"

"I don't know the titles of the songs, but I love the music. Sometimes I come to the cathedral on Sunday to listen to the priest. Every now and then he has good words to live by."

"Are we dressed nice enough to be in a church?"

"Our appearance doesn't matter because no one will see us."

We went in a side door and up a staircase. Gabriel cranked the door open. "It's okay," he whispered as I went in first. "Take a look down." He led me to the open space. I took a look down. It was a beautiful cathedral. The rows of seats seemed like they went back for miles. The windows were painted with Biblical stories.

"You read the Bible?" I inquired.

"It's the only thing that keeps me going. My mum used to read it to me before I went to sleep. She loved that book. Reading it makes me feel close to her. I would sit right here." Gabriel showed me the spot he sat at. "And read it while the bells played. The music makes all the stories come to life. It's a great book."

"What book will you read next?"

"This is the only book I read."

"Well, you should consider reading others as well."

"Are you a believer?"

"If it means I'll be able to be close to my mum, then yes, I am. Are you?"

"I'm not a believer."

Gabriel was lying down. I lay next to him. We listened to the bell ring. "You think I'm going to hell because I don't believe?"

"God will forgive you. I heard him forgive murderers and rapists. Just ask Mary and she'll relate the question."

"We're all unpure," is what read on the ceiling.

"You think that's true?"

"It has to be, according to the stories."

"Then no one should be judged."

"I try not to judge people, but sometimes they do the most stupid things and deserve to be judged for it."

I looked at him. "How may I help you?" I asked.

"This is my secret place. Thank you for coming here with me."

"You think your mother is here?"

"She's everywhere," he said, looking back at the sign.

"I lived in New York before I moved to Paris."

"You miss it?"

"I only miss Ms. Hickens."

"She probably misses you, too. You should call her."

"I may do that." I smiled, staring at the sign above. We stayed lying there for a time longer. We left taking another way out. A hallway decorated with paintings of local artists filled the walls.

"This is what I wanted you to see." Gabriel admired the work. "I want my work to hang on these walls."

"Why the delay?"

"A part of me doesn't think my work is up to the buyer's standards."

"That's silly. Your work is great. You're a lot more talented than some of the work hanging here."

"You really think so?"

"I do," I told him.

"Maybe I'll talk to the director to see how I would get started."

"You should do that," I encouraged. We left the cathedral walking side by side.

"I want to hear you tell me you'll be proud of me when a buyer buys a painting of mine," he said.

"I will be. I am proud of you for starting a painting buyers will buy."

"I'm proud of you for keeping your back straight," he said. "You look good with it that way." I allowed him to walk a little ahead of me. Feeling as good as I looked, "Are you coming?"

I hopped to Gabriel. "Yes," I flirted with him. We walked the streets arm in arm. We ate a lot of chocolate.

"Will you be over tomorrow?" he asked.

"Tomorrow is my last day for my summer class. Mr. Borax will be giving out reviews and who he thinks will make a good head chef. I've pleased him the whole four weeks of the class. I got a good feeling about tomorrow, but I don't want to get too excited."

"He would be insane not to give the position to you," he flattered me.

We parted ways. Before I got too far, I called back to Gabriel, "Maybe one day you wouldn't mind taking me to church with you."

"To hear the priest speak?" he called back.

"Yes!"

"It's a date, Bellina!"

"So it is, Gabriel." My angel Gabriel, I thought. That was our first date.

Summer was gone, my summer class ended soon. The saying had always said all good things must come to an end. The ten of us waited for Mr. Borax to read our reviews. He decided to sit with us one by one for recommendations. People not connected to the institute were first. I tried not to be too serious. I shrugged. I knew this class wouldn't make or break my career, but it was still a close bet.

"Bellina, I'm ready for you." He called me in. I left my station to enter his white door. "Have a seat." He pointed to the seat in front of his desk. I sat eager to know if the dream I had strived for was about to become a reality.

"You've impressed me this month. If you keep working with different things and challenging yourself, I think you could become a great chef. The committee will know how I feel and strongly consider my recommendations. I'm proud of you and glad to be telling you that you've earned my recommendation for head chef. Congratulations,"

I leaped into the air from seat. "Thank you!" I cried out. "Yes, oh thank you," I cried joyfully. Mr. Borax smiled. I knew he understood my enthusiasm.

"Now, that doesn't mean you got it, but it means you're on your way to having it," he told me.

"I know, Sir. It means I'm strongly on my way to becoming it." I repeated the effect he had with the school committee. I shook his hand and I was free to go. Head chef was mine, I could just taste it. I could feel what my fourth year was going to be like.

The restaurant was going to set standards beyond the expected expectations the school set and former head chefs created. I wanted to bring something to the table no one had before. I hoped they were ready for me. I arrived at the shop with my brain exploding from thoughts of running the school's restaurant. The grin on my face hadn't left it.

I grinned all the way home until I turned the corner and my grin slowly fell apart. Luc paced back and forth in front of the shop's door.

"What are you doing here?" I mouthed loudly.

"That's the million dollar question; I've been asking myself since I got here. How did I manage to come back here? Well, I was walking around and here I am." He threw his arms helplessly into the air. The time had been long, but short enough from when we last saw each other.

"I have thought about you a lot," I confessed.

He smirked an unbelievable smile, "You've thought about me, but couldn't come after me," he said. His response struck anger inside of me.

"You were the one who left me!" I stated.

"I know, I just thought that deep down you did love me and would come for me." He stood there with his hands on his hips; he didn't know where to look. "Okay, I'm sorry, I'll leave now."

"Wait, please," I said as I choked up, reaching for his hand. "I'm the one who should be sorry." It was true. My feelings grew stronger for Luc during the time we were apart.

"And you still couldn't come by the café?"

"I can only say I'm sorry and see if you want to move forward with me." I expected the answer would be yes but the uncertainly in his face made me unsure. "I love you," I added in hope he would change his mind.

"Say it again," he said.

I smiled. "I love you," I told him. I stood on my tippy toes to kiss his cheek. Before I could kiss him, he scooped me up, wrapping his arms around me. We stayed like that for a while.

"I have a surprise for you."

"I am surprised," I said happily.

"Not yet. I've not surprised you yet, but come with me and I'll be happy to give you a surprise you'll love." He held out both hands for me to take.

"Where are we going?" I asked.

"If I tell you it would not be a surprise."

"Give me a little hint."

"Would you like to come with me on a road trip?"

"Okay," I agreed just like that. He smiled, taking my hands. Luc had rented a car. The car wasn't as big as Ms. Hickens', but I was in Paris, and in Paris there are small cars. I laughed at the thought of comparing cars. Luc got into the car, then turned to me and kissed me. I missed his soft lips. I had to admit it felt good to surrender.

"Are you going to tell me anything?" I was excited.

"It's a surprise," he teased, "Here's a hint,"

"What?"

"You're going to love it," he confidently said.

We drove out of the city, passing trees and older homes. My luck grew in a day. This morning I accomplished achieving my goal, this evening Luc forgave me. I was lucky. I enjoyed the scenery of the green grass blowing left, then right, from the breeze of cars driving by.

"Where are we going?" Luc had pulled into a small cafe. It was almost in the middle of nowhere.

"I told you, it's a surprise."

"How may I help you two?" An older woman came to the counter. *We make the best cup of coffee* was printed on the sign behind her.

"I'll have your best cup of coffee,"
Luc said.

"I will, too."

"And to eat?"

"We're fine, thank you."

The woman went to get our coffees.
There were a few other people in the cafe.
"I wish you would tell me," I told him.

"And kill the fun? I don't think so."
We sat across from each other. "You know
every time you sit across from me, it
feels like you're too far away."

"I promise you I'm not." I smiled.
"You're still not going to tell me?"

"No!" He laughed. We drank our
coffees. "Wait, you have to wear this and
I'll take it off once we get to where
we're going."

"Luc!" I protested.

"Put it on for me, please." He kissed
me for a long time before letting me go. I
smiled as he blinded me with a cloth so I
couldn't see the rest of the trip. I
depended on my sense of smell to bring
some kind of visual to my mind. The smell
of fresh flowers and food told me we were
in a town. The drive had us traveling for
what seemed like hundreds of miles. The
rain came slowly down.

I held out my hand to feel it falling
on my skin. I loved the sound of
raindrops; they reminded me of my father.
When we finally stopped, I was stuck in
the position I had been sitting in. My
legs had given out from the long drive.

"Can we just stay here for a second longer? I can't move," I told Luc.

He laughed, trying to ease my arms loose from around him. "Then your muscles will stay tight."

"Ohhh," I moaned

"Shake your body." Luc helped me out of the car. I was still blindfolded standing, shaking my muscles to help the blood flow through my body. "Shake like crazy." Luc laughed, probably at the sight of me. I stepped forward and collapsed, "Woohh, take it easy." He guided me in a circle. "When we go home, remind me to take a couple of breaks along the way," he joked.

"I will! Are you going to tell me where we are now?"

"I'll do better. I'll show you." He let go of my hands and came behind me, pulling off the blindfold. The bright sunshine made my eyes blink. I turned quickly to Luc; he'd brought me to my childhood home. Words couldn't explain how surprised I was or how lucky I truly felt. The home looked exactly the same as I left it.

The garden grew trees with new fruit on them. The grass was green as ever. The place reminded me of dancing with my mother. She danced in a silk, white sundress, twirling as the wind, blew her around. My father was near fixing his car; he fell in love with his car, while he was in New York. "Don't leave the oil in the yard," my mother warned him.

"I'm not, Beautiful. I promise," he said. She smiled his way. He stopped to watch her finish her dance. "Bellina, you want to learn about cars?"

"Yes," I said smiling at him.

"Come on; let me teach you before you get too old."

I laughed. "Don't you mean before your car gets too old?"

"Impossible. This car will stay young forever." I ran to learn about cars. The day looked like today, beautiful, shiny and like a dream. I missed this place. It kept my dreams, and for that I was thankful. The house looked like it had been repainted. They stood in front of the door too afraid to come closer. I couldn't believe my own eyes.

"Surprise, my love," Luc whispered in my ear. Surprise wasn't the word to describe that moment; no word could.

"Tom… Claudia," I cried as I stumbled before I ran into their arms.

"Bellina, we missed you so," Claudia cried. Our arms were wrapped around each other.

"Let me see you." Tom looked at me. "You're even more beautiful than Luc said."

"Come in, come in, we left everything the way it was." Claudia led me in. Tom and Luc followed.

"Oh my," I whispered in surprise. Everything was the same as the day I had left. The photos were untouched. They welcomed me in.

"Sit down." Claudia sat me down. "No, stand up. I want to see you." I stood back up. "I made you everything you love, tried to, by the way." Claudia looked at Luc. "Bellina's mother was the cook. Oh, my, you look just like her," she said to me. "She would have been real proud to see the young woman you turned out to me. Now tell me, Luc said you're in Paris getting a culinary degree. Maybe you should have cooked for us." We all laughed.

"Yes, I'm the head chef for my last year. I just found out. Wow, I missed you." I hugged Claudia, like I would never let her go.

"I thought I would never see this day," she said.

"Do you two have children?" I asked.

"No," Claudia's voice saddened. "Work and travel took over our lives, but it's okay. We got you back."

"Claudia, Luc and Bellina must be starving. Let's get these kids something to eat," Tom said.

"Oh, I wouldn't want it to get cold." Claudia and I held each other as we walked into the kitchen; I ate at the same place as when I was a little girl.

"Oh, can we take our meals outside and eat in the garden?" I asked.

"What a lovely idea, of course." We took our plates of food and glasses of juice outside into the sun.

"You have quite the young man, Bellina." Tom took a liking to Luc. They became friends.

"Tell us how you like Paris." Claudia sat next to me with her plate of food in her lap.

"Claudia, you know how Paris is."

"I want to hear it from you. I'm so happy you have the chance to travel. I didn't think." Claudia stopped her sentence. She looked at her plate.

"You did not think what?" I asked. "She wouldn't allow me to travel?" The mood changed. I was sure they knew my conditions. Sadly there was nothing they could do to stop it.

"That doesn't matter now. You're safe and surrounded by people who love you." Luc lightened the mood back to the joyful feeling we all felt.

"I couldn't have said it better," Tom added. They were right, only now mattered. We watched the sun set, sitting in a circle. I yawned from the long day's drive.

"You should be headed to bed; every woman needs her beauty sleep," Claudia said.

"I don't have any overnight clothes," I said.

"Here, I packed you a bag before I got you," Luc confessed, giving me my overnight bag, "See, I told you not to worry. We took care of everything. You just have to be here."

"Thank God you are," Claudia said. "Let's unpack in your room." I wanted to sleep downstairs in the living room. After the long ride, I knew we needed a bed to sleep on. The door was open. "Oh, my doll." My mother bought me the golden china doll on her trip to Syria. She had put it away so it would preserve its likeness.

"Ohh," I sighed as I flopped onto my bed with the doll in my arms.

"I come here every day and pray for your safe return," Claudia told me. "You know, the word *angel* is used and tossed out of people's vocabulary like it means nothing, but I truly know God has sent one to me and answered my prayers." We held each other. "My child died in childbirth months after you left. I couldn't take all of the stuff that was going on. I was physically and mentally too weak to fight to get you back. Tom and I have had many battles; it's only through God that we're still together."

"Were you fighting over me?"

"No, my love." She kissed my head. "Oh, Tom and I never fought over you. We love you too much for that. Our battles were over small stuff. But all have been fixed. Now that Luc has brought you back to us, I can stop my tears from shedding in this house."

"You know about my aunt, that she's my birth mother?" I sparked the question I had never discussed with anyone. Claudia's face said it all; she looked as if she was shocked by an electric wire. "I found the letters she wrote to my mother and father. She wrote often how she couldn't go on without him." I looked around the room I had once pretended to be sleep in. "Do you know who he is?" I had a million questions buried inside of me.

"Yes, please don't hate us for it. We all vowed to keep it a secret to protect you. Your mother wanted to help her sister. Instead of receiving the help we offered, she turned back to drinking and sleeping with strange men. Your mother and father had enough of it and finally cut her off. They did it with only you in mind. You were so tiny when you were born. It didn't matter who was in the room, you let us hold you. It felt so right because you trusted us. Keeping that secret was worth it. Now you have to forgive us for it and not let it hold you back." She pleaded, "I've never met the man or your birth father. I'm guessing he's the him she couldn't live without."

"I'm so upset," I said, grinding my teeth together.

"Oh, Bellina, forgive. It's the only way your heart won't hurt anymore. I've learned it's the most powerful act to do. I know it doesn't happen overnight; it takes more time to put everything awful that happened to you at rest. But once you do, you'll never have a more fulfilling life."

"Who have you forgiven?" I wanted to know. Her tears fell on me while mine fell on the bed. We both were trying to let go of the past and move forward to the future.

"It took me a while to forgive God for allowing your mother to die. She was my best friend; we were going to be old ladies, drinking lemon tea and eating small cakes in the garden next to the pond. I hated him for never blessing me with children and taking you away. Most important, I hated him for how I felt."

"You think he made your life worse for hating him?" I asked with tears in my eyes.

"No, he didn't. He was patient with me. He allowed me to come to him on my time and he comforted me as I cried in his hands. Together, he and I took care of me. Now that I've forgiven, he blessed me by bringing you here and Luc. Tom and I just adore him. No matter, what you keep him. Beautiful babies I see you two having."

I laughed, "He is kind of special."

Luc knocked on the door. "Am I disturbing you? I can go back downstairs."

"No, we're finished. The both of you should get some sleep." Claudia got up. Tom came into the room. "Oh, beautiful," He hugged me. We laughed, staring at each other. "I love you!" He said, "Tomorrow is

going to be a great day. Get plenty of
rest; I can't wait to show the both of you
around."

I kissed Tom and Claudia goodnight.
Luc and I lay in bed once we heard the
door shut behind them.

"Wow, how did you do this?" I asked,
amazed that he would do this for me.

"I'll tell you tomorrow at lunch. I
want you to sleep with the look you have
now on your face." It didn't take us long
to fall asleep. I forgot about Gabriel,
but I was long gone. There was nothing I
could do about it. I was in my bed, in my
room, in my house; I was so happy.

* * *

"Good morning sleepy beauty and beau.
I made your breakfast." Claudia was
slicing fruit.

"I'll be back down in a few. Don't
wait on me to begin eating." I hopped
upstairs, charging into my mother's
bathroom. Her towel hung over the tub. Her
perfume was still filled in bottles we
brought long ago. I started the tub. The
hot water ran down my hand. I poured my
mother's favorite bath bubbles in it. I
was going to soak in the bath and let my
thoughts come to glory.

"Hello." Luc came in.

"What are you doing in here?" I asked.

"I came to bring you your breakfast. You can indulge while you bathe." He set my plate on the table next to the tub.

"Thank you."

"I'll be out in the yard with Tom. Claudia is cleaning the kitchen. Don't be in for too long. We have the whole day planned."

"I won't."

"Did you save me any hot water?" he joked.

"Of course!"

"Ha." He closed the door behind him, leaving me to indulge in the plate of food that smelled so good and back to my glory of thoughts.

* * *

Introducing Amelia Mon Belle

"Sir, Lady Amelia has arrived, Sir." The server of the night alerted the manager.

"Thank you; please give Lady Amelia an ocean view table. I want her to have the best dish the chef has to offer." The manager of the restaurant said.

I took my seat. Couples danced to the jazz that played seductive songs. The server poured sparkling cider for me. He put a bowl of bread on the table.

"Lady Amelia, the chef prepared his a special meal for you." The server told me.

"Yes I did." The chef appeared by the server. "I wanted to come over here personally to shake hands and honor another chef." He said.

"Oh one day I would love to invite you to my restaurant to honor you," I said.

"One day I'll take you up on your offer," he said. We chatted and then he left, as I indulged in the courses he made just for me. At the end of our night, he took off his chef's jacket and put on his former black tux.

"Lady Amelia," he said.

"Yes," I answered.

"May I have this dance?" He held out his hand. We danced in the centered of a crowd that spectated in awe. The night had been grand.

*　*　*

I splashed in the tub to keep the heat from leaving the water. It would be grand to be an honor chef. I would always be a lady.

"Bellina, are you alright?" Claudia called.

"Yes, I'll be out in a minute," I answered her.

"Okay, I was just checking."

There was no doubt in my mind, I was safe and secure. I dipped my head in the water.

"Ohhh, surprise, surprise." The lavender soap was in the soap dish. I took it. I closed my eyes and caressed my body with it. I felt wonderful. I gently rubbed the cloth on my skin. The dirt was leaving and so was my guilt. I rinsed off the soap and dirt I had on me. A puff towel waited for me to cuddle in. I held it like it was holding me. "Hmmm." I stood there for a while to feel the warmth from the towel's thickness. I went to my room. Luc had put out my clothes. He had good taste.

"Welcome down, stranger," Tom greeted me.

"I had to freshen." I washed the plate. "Claudia, the breakfast was great. I think you should be my instructor for this year."

"Oh, I would love to!" she said.

"Have you all eaten?" I asked

"Yes, I'll go shower and we can begin our day." Luc kissed me as he ran upstairs. Tom winked at me.

"Tom, you're looking good," I told him.

"I'm making up for my school days," he said laughing.

"Finally, I knew the day would come," Claudia teased. I laughed.

"How is the bank, Tom?"

"Brilliant, A couple of years ago, it took off. I found a wonderful partner who's the closest business partner I have to your father." He kissed Claudia.

"What?" I was shocked. "Claudia?"

"Yes! I'm his partner in crime."

"And she loves every minute of it," Tom said. "We remodeled it."

"It's chic, contemporary, thanks to my fashion sense," Claudia praised herself. "Oh, I want you to see it."

After my father's murder, I never went back to the spot he was killed. Going there was something I had to do because I didn't go to his murderer's trial. One thing I did know was my father's murderer was still in jail.

"Thank God for justice," Claudia said.

I looked at her. Yes, thank God, I mouthed. She nodded okay, that I needed my time to find my peace with God.

"I'm ready to go," Luc proclaimed.

"So are we," said Tom.

"Where are we going?" I asked.

"First stop to the back and around town," Luc said.

"Lead the way," I said.

The bank looked incredible from the exterior. It had grown with the years.

"Wait until you see the inside." Claudia opened the door. I went in without seeing the spot where my father laid. The inside was stylish. The walls were painted a grey shade. French doors opened to glass tables stabilized by red legs. A pair of sofas and chairs made the center the lobby, and a little bar hosted drinks.

"We have an upstairs, too. My office is right next to Tom's, only mine is bigger," Claudia boasted.

"I absolutely love the rugs and the art on the walls," I said.

"We wanted it to be local but still have an international feel for all of our international customers. We're getting rave reviews from China to the States."

"I'm so happy for you." I hugged Claudia. A memorial of my father hung on the wall. He never looked more handsome.

"That's my father," I showed Luc.

"It's a pleasure to reunite you with him."

"Well, you two crazy kids, we have to stay here to fix a minor detail before it turns out to be a major one."

"Ahhh," I sighed

"Oh, go have lunch without us. We'll catch up with you tonight." Claudia kissed us both. "I insist you go and have a wonderful time."

"If you insist, we must do as we're told," Luc said.

"I believe you set this up," I said to Luc. He smiled. We left the back.

"Wait, this is where it happened." The spot my father was shot. We looked at it. "I know what I can do." I went back to the bank's door.

"What are you doing?"

I walked on the spot to the end of the sidewalk, then I walked back. I took Luc's arm. "Now we can move on." We both walked over the spot and kept walking. We found an Italian restaurant not too far from the bank.

"I am craving pizza," Luc said.

"One pizza it is," I agreed. Our pizza came hot with a ton of cheese on it.

"The Swiss did well," Luc joked.

"I'm sure you'll eat anything."

"I would," he said. I ate my slice and we sat there.

"Luc, when did you plan this?" I finally asked.

"I thought you were upset at me for going through the letters. I looked at you and thought I lost you. I searched for Tom and Claudia last week. I came here to see them. To make sure they were the real deal. I saw everything; it made sense. I saw the house and the garden, and your face appeared. Claudia burst in tears when I came."

I laughed, knowing how emotional Claudia could become. "Everything fit, and Tom told me it may seem things can't be too good to be true, but some things really are."

"Like you; you seem too good to be true,"

"I love you. I would do anything for you."

"I know you do."

"Do you love me?" Luc asked.

"I love you as strong as you love me," I sincerely told him. The joy in his eyes turned him pinkish red.

"Shall we go?" he asked.

"I'm ready." We pushed our way outside. How could I not love the man who made my dreams come true? I thought.

"May I hold your hand?" he asked me.

"Yes." He kissed my hand and held it on our way back to the bank.

"It has been my honor to reunite you with your other family. I would do it all over again to see the look you carried on your face. I hope it stays there. I love you and I just want to see you happy."

I teared up. "Thank you, Luc," I managed to cough out the words.

"No, thank you, Beautiful."

I had no idea what I did to have Luc in my life. He could have had any woman who would have been far more appreciative than I, one who didn't have the lack of self-confidence and abusive past. For some reason I was special to him and, like every good man, he became a knight.

Chapter 14

We started our day early. Claudia and I held each other for dear life. "You'll write to me?" Claudia persisted.

"Yes," I promised her.

"Because we'll be able to see each other often now. You're not so far away. Please bring back Luc. We can all get together for the holidays." Claudia sobbed.

"Of course," I sobbed, too.

"They have to get going before the storm comes in," Tom pointed out.

"Oh, I don't want you to leave."

"We'll see each other soon," I assured her. I ran to Tom. "I love you."

"I love you. Luc, take good care of her," Tom told Luc.

"I'll do my best, Tom." He hugged Claudia and Tom. We departed with me sobbing on Luc's neck. On our way home we took several stops. I walked around, glad Claudia and Tom had kept their promise. I could return home anytime.

"Here we are." Luc stopped in front of the shop.

"I can't thank you enough," I told him.

"It's okay, you already did."

"Luc, I want to confront my aunt, face to face," I said loud and clear, so I could hear the words.

He stared at me with a blank face. "I don't know if that's a good idea, love."

"Yes, I want to. Claudia gave me answers, but I want to hear it from my aunt. That way, for once, I could finally move on."

"What makes you think she will be around for you to see or change at all?" he asked me.

Only I didn't know the answer to his question. It may be I'll never get a chance to see her again. I knew I couldn't go searching for her. The chances of her coming to me were none. So, I had guessed I was at a misfortune of hearing the truth from her. "I love you, Bellina, my beautiful girl," Luc told me, then we drove off.

I went up to my studio and sat on bed. I thought about how lucky I was. I missed Geneva. I ran out of the shop to a pay phone. I was so excited.

"Ms. Hickens, Ms. Hickens," I screamed her name before she answered her phone.

"Bellina, honey, honey." Her tone was calm. She sounded worried.

"Ms. Hickens, you're not going to believe it."

"Bellina, Bellina. Oh, I've been trying to call you all week," her voice softly said.

"Ms. Hickens, what's wrong?" I didn't like her tone. She started to worry me. A million thoughts ran through my head. I was scared. "Is everything all right? Are you healthy? I can come home right now!" I cried out.

"Bellina, it's not me. I've been trying to reach you about-"

"What is it?" A near calmness came to me. It wasn't Ms. Hickens; she was fine. I couldn't figure out why her voice was shaking and stressful. The thought something was bothering her made my stomach sick.

"Bellina, Baby, it's your aunt." There was a silence between us. I wanted to hang up the phone. "Bellina, Bellina, are you there?"

"Yes, I'm here." I choked the words out.

"Your aunt may not make it much longer. She's at the hospital. She's been calling for you."

The chance I thought I would never get came from nowhere. Maybe Claudia was right; God does hear you.

"What is wrong with her?" I didn't need anyone to tell me; I knew the answer. Her body had given up on searching for her next drink. It was tired.

"She is dying of cancer. She's been asking to see you."

We sat on the phone in silence for a long time. Now that I got what I asked for, I didn't know if I wanted it.

"Well," I repeated, "would you have come if you were in my shoes?"

"Honey, I can't answer that. I think you should come to say your peace. I'll support you if you decide not to come. But either way, you have to do what your soul says feels good." She gasped. "You have nothing to feel guilty about."

"This fall I'm going to be head chef. I got it!" I whispered a cry out. "I don't want to give it up, at least not for her."

"That's fine, baby. I know this is a lot thrown on you all at once, but remember, there's not a lot of time your aunt has left. You don't want her to leave our world without saying your peace."

"Umm, I have to go; I'll talk to you later." I quickly hung the phone up. I ran to see Gabriel leaving my studio unlocked. Luc was working and didn't get off to late, and I needed someone to talk to at that moment.

"Gabriel!" I ran up the stairs and into his place.

"Was this the tomorrow you were talking about?" He wasn't pleased.

"I've just been taking off a roller coaster. I reunited with my family in Switzerland, and my aunt is dying in the States."

"I'm sorry for your roller coaster ride." His voice was plain, as if his work had been ineffective by my absence.

"I'm sorry but so much has happened. I may have to leave to go back to the

states. I may have to give up becoming
head chef if I leave," I said in
disbelief.

"What will you do?" he asked me.

"I don't know I'm stuck in an
unfortunate middle. Gabriel, I may have to
give up my dream."

"You don't have to give it up. You
have to figure which is the most important
and put the other on hold."

"My aunt is my birth mother. I found
out in a pile of scattered letters. This
may be my only chance to have closure from
her," I said doubtfully.

"Then go to her. You'll always have
cooking. You're a great chef. Maybe you
can make it home before the semester
begins. After all, you don't owe this
woman your life." He was right.

I looked around his studio. "I'm so
sorry I caused you to ruin your painting."

"It's not ruined, I finished it. The
most important part was done."

"The most important part?" I
interrupted.

"Painting you," he told me. "There it
is." He pointed behind me. There I was,
painted looking out a lone window
surrounded by bright colored roses.

"It's so beautiful," I said.

"It's a gift for you to keep." I
turned to him, surprised. "Don't worry, I
sold another painting."

"Wow, thank you," I gratefully told him. Not only did I take the painting, I took the advice he gave with me.

That night, I hid under the covers, hoping to escape the world. I flipped from the top to the bottom. She called for me on her death bed. We were past the acts in the plays. The chapter was over. The rain had finally started to fall, but I could still see the stars in the sky.

"Claudia," I called her.

"Bellina. Oh, I'm so happy to hear from you so soon. I wish you were still here. I started not to let you go." She laughed.

"I wish you hadn't. Uh, Claudia, I received a call. Aunt Michelle isn't doing so well. She's in the hospital," I told her.

"Oh, I'm sorry to hear that," she said, "Wow, all this time has finally caught up with her."

"She's calling for me. What should I do?"

"Oh, Bellina, if it was that simple. You need closure. She's the only one who is able to give that to you."

"I realize that, I just don't know if I can handle it," I said.

"You can. You are a strong girl. Go and make your closure," she told me.

"I wish you were here," I told her.

"So do I."

"I must go."

"Call me and let me know what you decided," she said.

"I will, of course." We said our goodbyes and I laid down thinking; I was going back to New York.

The next day, I walked to the café. I had to see Luc before I left. I needed him to tell me everything was going to be alright. I needed him to let me know he was going to wait for my return.

"Hello, Beautiful, I can see written all on your face, what is wrong," he sincerely asked me, sitting down with me at the corner table.

"She actually has called my name to see her," I told him. The look of uncertainly came into his eyes.

"What happened?" he asked.

"She's dying of cancer and Ms. Hickens called to alert me."

"Are you going back?" he said as he choked his words.

"Yes, I'm leaving tomorrow," I told him.

"Will you come back?" he fished for answers.

"Yes, I will be there for a week. I have no plans of missing my last year of school," I said. Luc looked at me as if I was missing another important part. "And you," I added. "I got to go home and pack. Will you take me to the airport?"

"I will after breakfast," he said smiling.

From the café, to my studio felt like I traveled it alone. The roads were gray and the world was black. I started to run to a phone to hear a kind voice.

"Ms. Hickens, it's me!"

"Bellina, oh love, how are you feeling?"

"Awful." I kept my eyes shut. I didn't want to see the world's darkness.

"Oh, honey, what you're feeling won't last. You have all this burden right now. Things will ease in time."

"How do you know that?" I asked.

"Honey, if you trust in God, anything is possible. You just let him take care of it," she assured me. I held the phone tightly to my ear. "Ohhh, honey, don't cry. We're going to get through this."

"What if I go to her and she's cold-hearted to me?" I thought out loud.

"All you worry about doing is saying your peace." She said it as if it was the easiest thing in the world.

"Yeah, but what if?"

"I know she won't be cold-hearted. This time she needs you to be the strong one."

"I can do that," I said strongly.

"The role has reversed now. You have to show your aunt mercy. She's dying; she can't hurt you anymore," she said.

"Okay, I need to pack. My plane leaves tomorrow."

"I'll pick you up from the airport. Rest now; I love you, Bellina."

"I love you, too." I went up to my studio. My eyes were wide awake until I fell asleep. Before I knew it, morning had come. Luc was knocking at my door.

"Here we go," I said sleepily. I was unrested. We ate our breakfast at the café and he waited with me until the flight attendant announcement came on.

"Flight 253 now boarding for New York," the speaker announced my flight.

"I'll call you as soon as I get to Ms. Hickens' house," I promised Luc, hugging him as tight as a person could hug someone. We kissed as people rushed past us.

"I'll keep by the phone then. I love you."

"I love you, too," I told him as the announcement came on again. "I must go." Luc nodded and kissed me again.

"Goodbye," I said, picking up my bag.

"Bye." We kissed one more time, then I got lost in the crowd of travelers moving forward. I looked back. Luc waved at me, blowing me a kiss, smiling. The temptation to stay was too strong, so I blew a kiss back and left, not looking back. Claudia and Tom said they would pack my things and keep it in Geneva. I had my personal items in a handbag, so I wouldn't have to pay for the extra bags. The flight over looked the same as it did my first time flying, only this time I didn't want to go home with anyone. I was traveling to a place I now knew.

"Ohhh, Bellina." I flew into Ms.
Hickens' arms, "You look so good," she
told me.

"I missed you so much," I told her.

"I know. I've missed you, too. You
should get your bags."

"I only have one." I grabbed my bag
from the baggage claim. "Let's go." We
left the airport. "Not a lot has changed?"
I noticed.

"Well, honey, you haven't been gone
that long."

"It feels like forever." We made it
to her home. "Oh, how I missed this
place." I darted inside. "Hmmm, it smells
like spice cider," I said out loud. I sat
on the couch, holding the pillow like a
little girl.

"Would you like me to take you to the
hospital?"

"Tomorrow; we'll go tomorrow. Let's
just enjoy today," I told her, happy to be
in her home.

"I have your favorite muffins." Ms.
Hickens went into the kitchen, bringing
out a tray of muffins.

"I know, I smelled them, too." I
dropped the pillow. The muffins were
waiting on me, topped with my favorite
caramel sauce.

"It's so nice to have you back in my
kitchen," she told me. It was more than
nice. *Home sweet home* read the mat under
the sink. Yes, I was. We set out to the
hospital early in the morning.

"After you left, she came back to the house. She'd been living there until she was found sleeping in the street," Ms. Hickens told me. "I recognized the name and went to the hospital to make sure it was her. She doesn't speak much. She looks much worse from the last you saw of her but be real gentle with her."

She pulled into the parking lot. I held my breath as we rode the elevator to the eighth floor. The smell of the hospital reminded me of an old folks' home. The sickness spread throughout the building. I tried to stop to turn around while I still had the chance. All the people behind me pushed me on. White coats, different from my chef jacket, flooded the hallways. It smelled like the angel of death made his home on this floor. Nothing could prepare me for walking through her door.

"We're visiting Michelle Hosset," Ms. Hickens told the overweight dark haired nurse.

"Sign in here." She held the sign in board to her face. "My God, don't mistake because my eyes are big that I can see well. I can't worth a dime these days," she joked. "Ah, here we go." She handed us the board. "Sign in here." She looked at me. "You must be the one she's been calling for."

I just looked at the nurse. She had big eyes, like she proclaimed.

"Michelle Hosset's room is down the hall, number 1478 on the left."

"Thank you," Ms. Hicken said. I started walking. "Bellina, why don't you go ahead? I'll be in the waiting room."

"You're not coming in with me?" I came back to her.

"You'll be fine. You and her need this time alone. I'll be right here, honey." She turned me around. "Go on, don't be frightened." She pushed me a little so I would walk. I looked back, hoping she would start walking with me. "Go on." She waved. I hesitated. "Go on," she said. I walked slowly down the long narrow hallway asking myself what I was doing here. I would rather be back in Paris. Room 1478 was right in front of me.

"Miss, are you okay?" A nurse asked me.

"Yes, I'm waiting to go in."

"Well, go on. I'm sure your family would love to see you." The nursed moved on. I took a deep breath before putting my hand out to open the door. There she was; her fragile body laid there. I couldn't tell if she was dead or sleeping. She was the only color in the room; everything else was white with metal and plastic running around it.

The surreal moment wasn't like what I had seen in the films. There was nothing the doctors could do, so all the tubes weren't stuck in her arms or choking down her throat. She lost all of her thinned hair and was bald. Her lips were chapped. She looked like a skeleton covered with skin.

"We took the feeding tube out because she was trying to bite it." A nurse came in.

"Okay," I quickly said. "How does she eat?" I wondered.

"We give her shots of food and liquid. She's stubborn and we don't have round the clock care for one patient. We do what we can." The nurse left. I sat on the edge of the chair waiting for her to awake in a rage. As she slept, she didn't look peaceful. I sat there thinking of the moment I stepped out of the cop's car and onto the steps of my aunt's door. I remembered the horrible smell and the roaches running in and out of the sink.

I rubbed my chin, remembering the first slap across my face she gave me due to her drunken rage. My arm still carried the scar from the fire of the cigarette that made my body freeze as the burning sensation traveled through my veins. I gaged thinking of all the cleaning I did, after she vomit everywhere in the house. I sat back holding the arms of the chairs to calm my stomach and settle my nerves as I tried to get the image of the vomit out of my head.

The more I tried holding tightly to the arms of the chair, the more uncontrollably my body shook as I thought of the time I peed on myself in front of

her, scared she was going to beat me with
a belt. Tears rolled down my cheek as I
couldn't hold it in. "How could you hurt
me like that? You beat your own daughter.
What monster does that to her daughter?" I
shouted angrily at her.

But she didn't do anything but sleep.
I felt better knowing she wasn't sleeping
peacefully. She slept as if death was
standing right next to her. Night fell,
and there was a knock on the room's door.
I fell asleep in the chair.

"Bellina, honey, are you ready to go?
You can come back tomorrow." Ms. Hickens
came in.

"I want to stay," I told her. I
thought I wanted to see more of her
suffering.

"Are you sure?" Ms. Hickens asked me.

"Yes, I want to be here." I gave her
a hug.

"Okay, I'll come get you tomorrow.
You have to shower and change your
clothes. Your aunt's status hasn't
changed. I don't think it will anytime
soon." I looked at her as she told me.

"I'll get cleaned up tomorrow, then
come back."

"Of course you will, baby." She
kissed me goodnight. "See you in the
morning." She left.

I sat back down, staring at the woman
who caused a lot of people pain. I
wondered who God will send to take her to
him. I wondered if he would forgive her,

what she would plead to him not to go to hell, and I wondered what she had to say to me.

"Bellina," she softly whispered my name. She was calling me in her sleep.

"Bellina," she whispered my name throughout the night. I listened to her whispers become quieter until she lipped my name, as if there was no one in the room to hear her. The ironic thing was she wasn't alone when she should be. I stayed with her the whole night watching her mouth my name. Ms. Hickens woke me when she arrived in the morning.

"Let's get you home to freshen up. See? I told you her condition hadn't changed," I looked at her; her lips were still moving.

"Yes, we should go," I said, getting up.

"We'll come back later," Ms. Hickens assured me. We left the hospital. Ms. Hickens had prepared a full breakfast. "You need fuel in your motor if you're going to be spending all those hours at the hospital."

"Should I eat first or take a bath?" I smiled.

"Take a bath. This food is going to be here."

"Alright." I went upstairs to take a bath. I never started the water; I ended up crashing on the bed. I had awakened up the next day with the sun beaming in my face.

"There she is. I'm glad you came home. You needed a good rest," Ms. Hickens said.

"I guess so; I just can't believe I missed your great breakfast you made for me."

"Oh, honey, don't worry, I made another for you." She did as I had showered. Omelets, sausage, muffins, orange juice and fruit filled the table.

"Are you expecting company?" I asked.

"You know me, I can't cook for two." She stared at me, fixing my plate. "You look like a woman."

"I feel like one," I told her.

"You are one," she said.

"Thanks to you."

"No, it took a village of women to make you one. You had three other preparers. Good or bad you learned, and we're all so proud of you." We finished our meal and headed to the hospital. My aunt had awakened and asked for me.

"Bellina." She tried to sit herself up. "Is that you?"

"Yes, it's me." I had grown taller since she'd last seen me. She'd forgotten what I looked like long before that night she abandoned me.

"Look at you. You're all grown up," she said softly.

"I'm a woman now." I made sure she knew.

"A very beautiful one," she added. The door opened and a nurse came in.

"It's time for your bath," said the nurse.

"Uhh," Aunt Michelle sighed. She was afraid to be touched. I went over to the nurse.

"Let me bathe her," I told the nurse. She hesitated to give me the bowl and cloth, but I held my hand up and insisted, "Please." The nurse handed me the bowl and cloth. "Thank you, you may leave now," I told her. I waited until she left to go over to my aunt.

I came here to get closure and move on with my life. With all of my anger built up inside, it all had been broken down and I felt sorry for her. She held her eyes closed, probably questioning how she allowed herself to lose all control. I fixed the bowl with soap and warm water. I removed her gown as gently as I could.

I didn't want to cause her anymore pain. I pulled her strings of hair away from her face. Then I dipped the cloth in the soapy water, rung it, and gently caressed her skin clean. I cleaned her as if she was my baby. I was as most careful as can be because her skin felt like it could be pulled right off. Her shame kept her quieted. It was alright because at the moment I had nothing kind to say to her. I carefully covered her in a fresh gown.

"Will brush my hair?" she asked me with a weakened voice. I looked down at her head; she had no hair brush. "Please, brush it," she pleaded to me. I picked up

the brush on the table and pretended to
brush her hair, softly brushing her skin.

"Have you eaten today?" I asked.

She said nothing. I went to the door,
peeked out of it and called to a nurse,
"Pardon me, can you please, bring a small
bowl of chicken soup and some orange
juice?" The nurse looked annoyed by my
question. "Please?" I asked again.

"If she doesn't eat it, then let us
handle our job with feeding her," she told
me, leaving unwillingly to get my request.

"From now on, I'll bring your food to
you," I told my aunt.

She opened her eyes and locked them
on me. "Why are you being so good to me?"

"I've always been good to you, even
when you burst in the house drunk,
vomiting over me. It was I who made sure
you were cleaned up. Even, after you beat
me." She turned and looked away.

"You made my body look like yours," I
told her, looking straight in her eye. The
nurse came in the room.

"Here's your chicken soup." She
looked as if she was telling me, why
bother, she's never going to eat it.

"Thank you," I told her, ignoring her
signals. "Here, it's hot and you need to
eat." I took the spoon and twirled the
soup around. "Slowly open your mouth." I
spooned the soup into her mouth. "Slowly
swallow it. You have to eat the noodles,
too."

"I can't chew." She opened her mouth to reveal she had lost all of her teeth. I tried not to look, disgusted by her appearance. She put her head down not to see my expression.

"That's fine. We'll just drink and I'll make you healthy food you can drink." I fed her the rest of the soup. "You need to drink the orange juice." I monitored her drinking the juice, making sure it went down her system smoothly. "There you go." I fluffed her pillow. "Do you feel a little better?" I asked.

"I do," she mumbled.

I got onto the bed and wrapped my arms around her. I stayed with her until she fell asleep from crying in my arms. It was my time to mother her. She had become my little girl. On my way out of the hospital I stopped to speak to the head nurse.

"Hello," I greeted her.

"Hi, how may I assist you?" the older, blondish woman asked me.

"I'm afraid my aunt isn't receiving the care she should be receiving. I don't want any more shots given to her for food. I'll be bringing her food from home. And if there are any more shots given to her, I'll report you all to the department of health. For now on, I'll be bathing her." I was firm with the nurse and left before she had the chance to speak.

"I'm so proud of you," Ms. Hickens proudly told me.

"Thank you," I said.

I spent as much time with my aunt as time allowed. Her color slowly came back.

"Are you going to eat again?" I asked her.

"No, thank you. Bellina, come here." I came to her, taking her hand. "I'm sorry. Sorry for everything."

"Sorry for what?" I knew what she was sorry for, but I wanted to hear her say so.

"Everything I did to you," she said with a scattered voice.

"I want to hear you tell me the things you did to me and that you're sorry for doing it."

She started to cough. I waited for her to stop. "After all the things you did to me!"

"You didn't want me there," she snapped at me, coughing heavily.

"I was a child!" I cried. "You took me from Claudia and Tom, only to hurt me. You got rid of me before," I cried to her. She looked at me as if death really did stand behind, "Yes, I know all about the letters. You got rid of me before; you didn't have to take me back."

"I thought I could, but I saw your looks at me, like I was nothing but a skinny, worthless, drunk. You were like the rest of them," she said, coughing.

"Then why did you take me?"

"I needed," She started to say.

"You needed the money to go get drunk!" I shouted. A nurse walked by and I calmed down. "I wanted you to love me and take care of me." I sat on the side of her bed. "I wanted you to be the woman in pearls I had dreamed about when I first met you." My tears fell on her.

"I could have never been that," she said. I knew she spoke the truth. In her mind she could have never been that woman I thought she was.

"Why not? You should have been for me!" I slapped the bed, crying. "You're supposed to want to be that." I heard the nurse come in as I cried.

"Is everything okay?" she asked.

"Yes," Aunt Michelle had slowly said, telling the nurse to leave. I felt her boney hands calm me. "I'm sorry for beating you and burning you. I was so ashamed of what I had done, of the life I had lived, I felt like I had no choice but to leave you. I was most afraid of the worst things I could do. Those things were my nightmares when I slept. But I can't go back and be that for you now."

I pulled myself up. "There's still time. We still have a little time. You're my mother," I said.

"Yes, you're mine." Teardrops fell from her eyes. We had lost a lot of time to make peace with the secret. Now it was said out loud. The clock ticked away. Our time was short as mother and daughter. "I

really like your food you made for me,"
she told me. I kissed her forehead.

"Thank you," I told her, "Can you
tell me who my father is?" I asked. Her
smile hindered around her face, "He was a
handsome man, my first love. His name is
Samuel Del Mar. You have his eyes. He is
American, a Frenchman at heart. I was in
college when we met.

He was my professor of French
Literature. I found out he was married
when I became pregnant with you. Your
grandparents were objective from the
start. They told me to leave. I dropped
out of school; started working at a bar
and my world has been painful since. You
were taken from me because I couldn't
provide you the life you deserved.

That's when Amelia…" She looked me in
the eyes. "Your aunt and I started writing
letters. They wanted to care for you,
while I pulled myself together, only I
didn't. I was devastated when the news
came of Amelia's death. My heart broke for
you, but I thought I could be the mother I
always wanted to be. Only I couldn't."

"Who knows why things happen. We can
change the ending, though," I told her.
The hardship from her eyes left. The next
two days, my mother's heath declined. I
made sure she was taken care of. I brought
her flowers and read her poems. I bathed
her the way I had learned to bathed
myself.

She was too weak to move so I would move for her, dancing around her room. I sang songs to my mother as she hmmm along. The past was the past; I wanted her to have peace. I brought out the piles of letters I carried. I read her the good ones between her and her sister. The letters made tears roll down her checks.

"Would you like me to stop?" I asked.

"No, please keep reading."

I read and read some more. The expression on her face changed.

"Those letters remind me that not everything between us were bad. I hope to see her waiting for me." She looked at the window. "Can you dance for me?"

"Yes." I put down the letters and danced around the room. I danced for the mother who raised me, the mother who taught me, and my new found mother. I danced for all of my mothers.

She died on a Sunday. Before they took her, I decorated her bed with beautiful lilies and French ivory pearls. Her departure hadn't been alone. I asked God to send his brightest fireflies to light her way to Him and to allow her soul to be free to travel the world and write her own poems.

I gave her one last kiss and gently brushed her skin. "You may take her now," I told the nurse. I had got my closure.

Ms. Hickens waited for me to come out the room. "How do you feel?"

"Much better. I know who my father
is."

"Will you find him?" she asked.

"I haven't made my mind up yet?" I
said doubtfully.

"When you're ready, you will." We
left the hospital.

"School starts in a couple of days. I
must be on my way," I told her.

"Oh yes, I'll be sad to see you go,
but you better," Ms. Hickens said
laughing.

I laughed, too. "This is my last
year. Will you visit? You can come eat at
the restaurant."

"I plan on it. I think springtime
would be a great time to visit."

* * *

When we arrived home, I couldn't take my
eyes off the house that held the worst
memories of my life.

"That's your house now," Ms. Hickens
told me.

"I want to sell it," I told her.

"I'm sure you do."

Ms. Hickens arranged for the realtor
to sell the house. The next day, I was on
a plane back to Paris. This time I was
leaving not to get away, but to finish
what I started.

At home, I phoned Claudia and Tom. "Hi, Bellina, how was New York?" Tom's voice shouted over the phone.

"It turned out good. I'm glad to be back in Paris," I said.

"That's good. Now, Claudia and I are glad you're back safe. We'll bring your stuff over this weekend, Hun."

I smiled. "I can't wait to see you guys."

"I'm happy now that you are," he said.

"Me, too."

"Claudia wants to speak to you." He handed the phone to her, "Bellina, it's me, Claudia. Baby, how are you doing?"

"Great, you were right. I'm glad I went back."

"That's wonderful. Bellina, you'll be alright," she told me.

"How do you know?"

"Honey, God told me in my prayers," she securely told me.

"Claudia, I'll talk to you soon. I'm going to get some sleep. Kiss Tom for me."

"I will." Claudia blew kisses to me. I blew kisses back.

"Good night, honey," she said.

"Goodnight."

Before I went to sleep, I thought of calling Luc but instead thought it would be better to surprise him at the café. In the morning I woke and took out a pen and paper writing a letter before getting out of bed. I wrote to God, I now understand the power of forgiveness and the power of love. Thank you for loving me.

Now, all three of you are my angels in heaven. Please watch over me. It's my prayer to God and I'll believe in him, if the three of you forgive each other. I know you're in a sky with millions of other angels, but the three of you were a family first; my family. Take care of each other and I'll be taken care of.

I kissed the letter, addressed it to my birth mother, my mother and my father. I sealed it and went to drop it into the mailbox. A car zoomed by. I smiled believing it was a signal. I rushed to get dressed so I could hurry to get to Luc.

I made it down to the fish shop's door when my phone started to ring. I hesitated at the door about whether I should answer it or keep going. It rang again. I ran up the stairs and threw open the door.

"Hello?" I answered.

"Well, I thought you were supposed to call me when you land?" Luc said.

"Luc!" I cried. "I'm sorry I forgot. Don't be upset. I'm on my way to the café now," I eagerly said.

"Don't go there. I'm not working today," he said.

"Oh, well, let's go out. I can't wait to tell you what happened. I have missed you," I said. Luc started laughing.

"We can't go out. I'm here, in New York," he said. It was like he dropped a bombshell on me.

"What?" I cried out, surprised.

"I wanted to surprise you after I didn't hear from you." He said, "I guess I couldn't be without you for too long."

I smiled, sitting on my bed astonished.

"I was going to surprise you at the café," I said, laughing with him.

"No need to now. I'm surprised you came back to Paris for me. I love you," he softly stated.

Me, too. I love you," I said smiling, feeling my life was complete.